UNION SOLDIER

In Gin Point, Iowa, the Union Army Enrolment Office is sifting through the locals for recruits. Jim McGaughey, a Harvard-educated doctor far from home, is determined to enlist, despite being exempt from the draft. When one young would-be soldier, roughed up by troopers, goes missing in suspicious circumstances, Jim — now a cavalry trooper — forms an alliance with the youth's sister, who is desperate to discover the truth. But enemies are lurking not only among the Confederates and Sioux, but within the ranks of Jim's blue-coated comrades themselves . . .

Books by Gordon Landsborough in the Linford Western Library:

THE BANDAGED RIDERS

GORDON LANDSBOROUGH

UNION SOLDIER

Complete and Unabridged

LINFORD
Leicester

First published in Great Britain in 1954
as *Union Soldier* by Mike M'Cracken

First Linford Edition
published 2016

*A catalogue record for this book is available
from the British Library.*

ISBN 978–1–4448–2790–3

Published by
F. A. Thorpe (Publishing)
Anstey, Leicestershire

Set by Words & Graphics Ltd.
Anstey, Leicestershire
Printed and bound in Great Britain by
T. J. International Ltd., Padstow, Cornwall

This book is printed on acid-free paper

1

There was an ugly sound, the sound of a fist upon bone. Someone fell, heavily.

Jim McGaughey wheeled, alert for danger immediately. He saw a man down in the dust of the broad street, saw three men in blue standing over him, saw people hurrying to get out of the way.

For a moment McGaughey thought to interfere. Then he shrugged. If he interfered in every brawl he witnessed he would have his fists permanently clenched.

The man got up. He was a civilian. He wore old jeans and a thick grey shirt that was now yellowed with dust. His worn, sweat-stained hat had come off. McGaughey saw a young face, a boy about twenty. The boy lifted his hand and touched his bruised cheekbone, hesitantly, as if the movement were not altogether under control.

He began to lurch away. As he went one of the blue-shirted peak-capped men lashed out and tried to kick him. He somehow evaded the blow and went headlong into the crowd, holding back to watch proceedings. Some of the people growled unpleasantly, their eyes hostile to the trio in the roadway. A woman's angry voice came from somewhere behind the spectators. McGaughey caught one word. 'Sojers — ' It wasn't complimentary.

He shrugged and turned to find the draft office. The three cavalrymen stood in the middle of the street, triumph intoxicating them. They were probably a little drunk anyway, McGaughey was thinking, though it wasn't yet noon. Most cavalrymen got drunk the moment they hit town. Then there was always trouble with the civilians.

As he walked down the street between featureless, unsightly clapboard buildings that never rose higher than two storeys, he realised that the trio were behind him. He looked over his shoulder as he walked.

They were being truculent. They were sizing up the crowd as they pushed through, looking for more trouble.

Watching the townspeople, those pioneers who had settled in Gin Point and made it a frontier town all within the last five years, with warring Indians and turbulent Nature against them, McGaughey thought, 'They won't stand for much more. They're not the kind.'

The war had been on too long now for the townspeople to retain many false illusions about soldiers. The glamour of those early days, when every blue-shirted Union soldier was a hero, had largely disappeared. Truculent, brawling soldiery had done that, mainly. Now the draft office was finally killing the last lingering dregs of sentiment.

McGaughey grinned to himself. Soon these civilians would be looking peevishly at him, too he thought. Very soon. This very day, most likely. Well, by the looks of things the recruiting regiment was cavalry and that was something. He never had liked walking on his own legs.

He stood aside to let the cavalrymen go past, watched them as they went by; hard men, blue-chinned and brutal. Men for whom the rigours of soldiering were acceptable if only because it saved them from that other hardship — daily toil.

They went on, pushing when people got in their way, swearing when citizens remonstrated, their hands lifting threateningly when words did not have their effect. McGaughey looked after them, and then the thought came to him: that wasn't just a brawl. There was something more to it than that, something behind that blow. But what?

He shrugged, walked on the street towards the river and the Enrolment Office. It was none of his business, he told himself.

* * *

His pulse quickened as he looked over the humming, active river, that tributary of the mighty Mississippi. Steamboats were everywhere on its surface, whistles tooting as they rounded the bend and came in to the crowded wharves.

The war in the South, the war so far disastrous to Northern hopes, demanded supplies, and from all Iowa they were pouring in. McGaughey stood with his foot resting on a barrel, enjoying the scene. Better make the best of it now, he was telling himself. He wouldn't be looking on it much longer.

Someone came and stood at his side but he took no notice. He was watching the riverboats loading. He saw the hundreds of barrels of pork and butter being rolled up the gangplanks, the sacks of beans, peas, wheat and oats . . . flour and sugar, crates of eggs and mountains of cheese; everything an army in the field needed.

A riverboat tootled on an uncertain whistle, its paddles revolved, churning up the mud; it reversed, turned and went scudding downstream. An empty boat standing out in midstream slowly turned her bows to take up the vacated berth. In that sunshine it was all rather jolly, almost exciting to watch . . .

Someone said, 'Why didn't you interfere? I saw you hesitating. I thought you would.'

Reluctantly his eyes came away from the river. As they trailed round he saw the Enrolment Office with its crowd of drafted citizens and the hangers-on who made profit out of the enrolment. Saw for one second three blue-shirted cavalrymen halted. They were looking his way.

A girl was by his side. She wasn't small, but against his own height she didn't seem big. Shapeless in the prevailing frontier fashion of long, cotton dress tied in at the waist and buttoned high at the neck. A bright dress, though, with defiant reds and blues that contrasted with the sober black of most other frontier women. Attractive to a man as young as Jim McGaughey, a man who didn't see much of women.

He saw brown eyes looking out from a face that was becoming flushed. Eyes that were hurt and angry, bewildered and desperate all at the same time.

She was holding her bonnet by the strings before her, her hands nervously playing with the bow. Hands, he saw, that were used to work; not white and slim and useless, but brown and strong and even roughened.

'I don't understand.' Faintly startled he took off his hat and stood staring down at her. The approaching river boat blew on its whistle and she waited until the sound had died before speaking. They stared at each other, his grey eyes perplexed — but approving. Hers wretched and angry and yet he knew, not with him.

Men were running along the wharf

towards them, their big, bare feet thudding hollowly on the thick rough planking. Professionally he noticed the flattened instep and thought, 'But it doesn't affect them. They work and run just as good as ever.'

The girl wouldn't have understood if she had known his thoughts. She said, her voice desperate, 'When they knocked . . . him down. In the street. Three against one and no one interfered. I was watching you and I thought you were going forward. But you didn't.'

Her voice was impatient with him. Jim McGaughey felt himself flushing with shame. Now he wished he had gone to help the civilian. Then those brown eyes might have looked more kindly at him.

The men were all around them now, hoarse voices calling to each other. They were hefting sacks and running towards the gangplank, just coming out from the riverboat. Hefting sacks and trundling barrels to fill yet another

Union supply ship.

* * *

McGaughey found himself going back to keep out of the activity. It pushed him against the girl, hard against the side of a dock shed that stank of oil and tarred rope. The hubbub was so great he almost had to shout down to her. Her face was no more than a couple of feet from his.

'I'd half a mind to kick in. But — ' He shrugged. ' — there's always brawling. It's sound sense in these parts to keep out of trouble.' It sounded lame. To his own ears he seemed to be making excuses and he didn't like it.

He was wanting to know why she had picked him out, a stranger. Why she should have been watching him in the first place. But those hot brown eyes tore away from his. She looked beyond him, along the crowded wharf. He thought she was near to tears in her desperation and he was bewildered.

'Three of them,' he heard her say, and he was sure her foot stamped under her long dress. The flush intensified on his brown face. Then he realised that the girl was staring at something behind him. He started to turn, felt the girl slip away round the corner of the hut.

Three men broke out of the crowd of dock labourers. Three men in cavalry blue. He saw blue chins, lowering faces, hostile eyes.

The man in the middle grabbed for McGaughey's shirt and caught him. Jim McGaughey saw a big, weathered, brutal face close to his, caught the stink of liquor on the trooper's breath. The other two men were crowding into him, hustling him against the untrimmed split log wall of the hut.

The man growled, 'Another of 'em. More'n we thought.'

Then one of the men kicked him. He gasped with the sickening pain of it and doubled instantly. The grip released on his shirt. The hand became a fist that chopped on to his unprotected neck. McGaughey went flat on his face, the rough, splintery wood of the wharf grazing the skin from his temple and cheekbone.

As he was rolling, someone drove a heavy boot into his ribs. Waves of pain swept over him, each wave seeming bigger, more painful than the last, driving him swiftly into the mists of unconsciousness. But he didn't quite pass out.

He heard distant men's voices shouting. Perhaps the wharf labourers'. But they wouldn't interfere against the army. Then that growling voice, full of dirt and evil menace — 'If it had bin dark you'd have got a knife in your ribs — you'd be in the Gin by now. So you know. Keep out of our way in the future. You an' them others . . . '

Boots tramped away. McGaughey moaned as breath came sucking into his lungs. His hand went down to the pain of that first brutal kick. He came slowly on to his knees, the sweat running into his pain-rimmed eyes, his breath gasping.

He began to recover. He saw bare feet and ankles under tattered cotton trousers standing around him. He lifted his head and said, 'Harvard wouldn't believe it,' and then wondered why he should have thought of that at that time.

He saw rough faces watching him. Eyes mostly curious, interested to see the extent of injury that a human form could endure. But one of the labourers spat angrily, 'Sojers!' his voice exactly matching that of the woman in the main street a few minutes before.

A raging bellow of a voice got the men back to work. Alone now, McGaughey pulled himself painfully upright against the rough timbers of the hut. His hair was damp with the sweat brought on by the pain. Gingerly he caressed a neck that felt broken. It hurt. He stood in the sunshine for many minutes and let himself recover.

All the time he was thinking, 'What

was that about?' These men couldn't know. It must be different. Then why had they attacked him?

'Because they saw me talking to that girl?'

That could be the only answer. Then what had those troopers against the girl — and her friends? His expert fingers explored his ribs. Bruised but probably nothing broken, he thought.

His eyes leapt with hot anger, recovering rapidly now. They sought for signs of the cavalrymen along the wharf, but they weren't there now. He wondered if they had gone in pursuit of the girl, and shivered. They weren't the kind of men to be left with a girl, any girl, much less a girl they hated.

Or was it they feared her? he thought, frowning. Fear and hatred. They were related in his experience.

2

He began to walk slowly along the wharf towards the Enrolment Office. That was where he had been told to report this day. The hot, early-summer sunshine made him want to be sick; it was too much on top of that thrashing, and all the time things swam before his eyes.

He kept on, though, looking for the cavalrymen. He didn't know what he would do when he met them; the only thing was that he knew he would do something.

'No, sir,' he whispered angrily to himself, holding the pain back in his stomach, 'they don't kick Jim McGaughey and get away with it!'

But they weren't anywhere on the wharves, neither were they on that busy street that fronted the river. He didn't like entering every saloon and grog shop in an effort to find them, and so gave up the search. He went across towards the Enrolment Office.

Outside the Council Building the hubbub was at its height. A long line of men dropped wearily in the sunshine, smoking, chewing and spitting, waiting to go in for examination. Down that length of queue, obstructing a broken board sidewalk that hadn't been repaired since a Confederate army first opened fire on Fort Sumter, smart-clothed men spoke softly to the draftees.

There were lawyers, ready to prepare affidavits proving alienage, non-residence, over-age for military service — anything. They were charging two hundred dollars a time, and there was no guarantee the affidavit would secure exemption.

And then there were doctors, eagerly offering medical certificates proving bad hearts, bad livers or anything else bad. They were charging what the public would stand and were doing a land office business.

McGaughey slumped at the tail of the queue against the clapboard Council Building. Other men were sitting on the hot sidewalk, some of them apparently dozing. A doctor came up, all smiles for the new customer. He wore a top hat, a pointed collar, a smart black suit.

'Get you out of this, mister,' he said confidentially.

McGaughey lifted his aching head and said, 'Don't want to get out of it.'

His head drooped, swimming and dizzy still. He wanted to have nothing to do with these damned quacks that got healthy, fit men out of the army, and made their fortunes at the same time.

The 'doctor' was persistent. 'They take heed of my certificates,' he whispered, looking furtively round. The man next to McGaughey had his knees drawn up, his head resting on his arms; looked to be sleeping. But there was no need for whispers,

McGaughey thought. Everyone knew what went on. The whole darned system was rotten and graft-ridden or the war would have been over by now.

'Reckon my reputation as a doctor is so mighty good, the surgeon won't even bother to examine you! Me, I've got so many off the draft — '

His voice was uncouth, not matching his slick, Eastern attire. McGaughey looked up suddenly and saw the pale blue pop eyes straining towards him, saw the bristly side whiskers and ragged fair moustache. Saw a stringy neck and wanted to wring it.

Temper drove away the pain and dizziness. His voice almost a snarl of ferocity, McGaughey snapped, 'Keep your dirty certificates. I'll bet you and that regimental surgeon go shares on all you make!'

Men were stirring along that line, looking towards the sound of the quarrel. Only the man squatting next to McGaughey seemed to slump deeper into sleep.

The pop eyes became prominent. But with the indignation was some unease. The quack began to say, 'That's a lie. You say that to the regimental surgeon when you get in — '

The rather quick, rather high, uncultured voice hesitated. The pop eyes were staring closely at McGaughey. Suddenly the quack said, 'I've seen you before. Back East, wasn't it?'

McGaughey's anger went out of him. He slumped against the wall. He said, 'Go away, darn yer!' And it seemed that his voice was deliberately coarsened, perhaps to disguise it. The man next to him stirred slightly, his head moving round so that one eye could peer towards McGaughey. He hadn't been asleep.

McGaughey got his tired head on to his knees, too. The quack began to walk away, looking for another reluctant draftee for a client. McGaughey got his head up to watch him go, saw the thin, ginger-whiskered face turn and look puzzled towards him. Like a man trying to stir his memory.

And McGaughey didn't want that memory stirring, not if they had met back East . . .

He found himself looking into the blue eye of the man next to him. Saw how covertly he was being watched over the crook of that grey-sleeved elbow. When their eyes met, that blue eye disappeared. McGaughey sat back, mentally scratching his head. He had come to Gin Point on the Gin River expecting to be out of trouble. But wherever he went, wherever he looked, queer disturbing things presented themselves.

The most disturbing thing, he thought almost humourously, was the thrashing he had received less than a half-hour earlier.

The queue shuffled in towards the door as a new batch went for examination. When his pain-wracked limbs were settled once more, McGaughey saw that his companion had resumed his squatting position.

McGaughey wished he had thought to look at the fellow's face, but he hadn't. Now it was buried in the grey sleeves again.

McGaughey let himself doze off into sleep. He knew that was what his bruises wanted — rest. And he knew they wouldn't get much of it in a little while. For about an hour he slept. Then, just before the next draft was taken in, his eyes opened. He saw he was being covertly watched again by that blue eye over the grey sleeve.

He was touchy, a bit raw with pain. Roughly he elbowed his companion and growled, 'What's the interest, fellar? What are you staring at?'

There was no answer from his companion, no movement. He squatted with his back to the wall, his head hidden again in his arms. McGaughey waited a second, heard the sounds of men at work all along the wharves, the voices of women shopping at Bird's Store next to the Council Building.

Then anger flared within him,

enraged at the deliberate silence of this man who had shown interest in him. Impulsively he knocked off the sweat-stained hat, grabbed a handful of dark hair and twisted the head towards him.

'Let's see your face,' McGaughey was growling. Then he saw it.

He saw a face that was curiously lop-sided. It was puffed up over the left cheekbone so that that distant eye had nearly disappeared in the swollen flesh. He saw a young face that was strained with pain, and it wasn't the agony of strongly clasped hair either, McGaughey realised. His eyes went back to that swollen cheek.

'You,' McGaughey exclaimed softly. It was the man who had been knocked down in the main street by that trio of cavalrymen. His anger evaporated immediately. Here was someone in a pain worse than his own, he recognised.

'I'm sorry,' he said. His fingers released their tight — too tight — hold upon the dark hair. The head slumped a little, the eyes drooping. 'Guess I'm kind of raw myself.'

But why was this stranger interested in him?

There was a stir then as a trooper with a list of names came to the door. The whole line stood up and began to shuffle forward through the doorway. The last batch of draftees came squeezing out with a lot of loud, cynical remarks. A sergeant came after them, shouting to them to keep quiet. Some horses were being brought up for the new recruits, but McGaughey passed inside the Council Buildings before he could witness the fun of those new troopers trying to mount.

They were in a dirty room, with a floor that was stained in ugly patches where the tobacco chewers had squirted. A brass cuspider stood to one side, but nobody seemed to use it. The draft stood around, waiting to be called for examination in an inner room. The talk was gloomy, mostly about the heavy Union defeats outside Richmond, Virginia. If they were accepted into the army now, for certain the whole blamed lot of 'em would be thrown into action against Lee and Stonewall Jackson before the month was out.

McGaughey had become separated from the man with the bruised face when they came in at the door. Now he saw him across the room and went across to speak to him. The man watched his approach apathetically. He was a sick man, McGaughey thought, his senses scattered by that vicious blow. He wondered about it, wondered about a lot of things. That girl with the despair in her angry bright eyes . . .

'I said I was sorry.' McGaughey braced his legs apart in front of the man. A trooper was calling men into that inner room. 'You've been hurt. Maybe I can do something to help you. But what I want to know is, why the interest in me? You kept looking.'

The younger man squinted through that puffy eye at the speaker. He saw a man still not thirty. A man. There was nothing youthful about McGaughey, though he wasn't coarsened into age by hard toil like so many others in that room. He had a good face, long and intelligent-looking, beardless and even without moustache. It made him look incisive, sharp, shrewd.

His eyes, grey as camp smoke in a morning, were sharp, too. Sharp, the younger man was thinking, but not cunning or unfriendly.

He stirred. His brain seemed hot and on fire. It seemed difficult to think, and it was getting worse. The face swam before him.

'I saw them. They beat you, too.' His voice was a whisper that was sharp-edged with pain. He caught his breath. 'What have you done agen 'em?'

He was swaying as he stood. McGaughey caught him, held him upright. The room was thinning. The officers were in a hurry to get to their messes and were running through the draftees with a speed that made a mockery of the word 'examination'.

McGaughey said, 'That should make us friends.' He tilted back that head, his hand under the beardless chin. He was examining the extent of the injury. But he said, 'Say, why did they do it to you?' It hadn't been an ordinary brawl, the lashing out of a drunkard upon a stranger. He had been sure of that from the start almost. And then, perhaps because that swaying youth didn't immediately answer he asked another question: 'Why did they go for me?'

The trooper in the doorway called out for three more men. McGaughey found he was among the batch to go in for examination. So was the injured youth. A broad, grinning man in the overalls of a farmer went in with them. As they went through the doorway he held up his right hand. Two fingers were missing. His expression was jubilant.

'Fust time I ever blest the axe that got them fingers. I ain't no good with a rifle! You see, I'll be out of that door in no time!'

That door was across the room from them. A knot of troopers were standing over by it to receive the accepted recruits. McGaughey, suddenly very weary of that morning in Gin Forks, saw a face staring at him. He had seen that face before — twice before. He didn't need to be told where.

As he looked, that incredulous face turned, whispered — and two more faces were beside his own. Three hard-faced, blue-chinned troopers gazed across the room, and McGaughey realised they were staring as hard at his companion as at himself.

A voice shouted loud enough to stir the dust in the room, 'Waken up thar! This ain't no the-ayter!'

A sergeant, bristling and important, was striding across the bare room. Three tables were in a line together, an officer and a trooper clerk behind each. The officers were lieutenants. To one side a heavy, middle-aged man wearing the uniform of a surgeon sat alone. He was taking snuff at that moment and making a mess of the operation.

The sergeant shouted, 'One man to each table.'

The three draftees dutifully moved across. McGaughey let his eyes flicker back toward the troopers. They weren't speaking, were still staring across at them as they halted by the tables. And McGaughey was certain there was no satisfaction on their faces; they looked instead like men who don't want to believe what they see with their eyes.

McGaughey turned at that towards the lieutenant. For the first time in quite a while he was feeling satisfied. It was something to know that his presence — or was it their presence, his and his companion's? — was disturbing to the troopers. After the hammering he had taken from them, it was some satisfaction.

The lieutenant was bored, wearied of seeing men out of uniform, faces that all seemed alike. Stupid faces, he was thinking languidly. Only stupid people had failed to get commissioned in the army by this time, was his thought.

'Name,' he snapped.

'McGaughey. James Clarke McGaughey.'

His head wasn't spinning any more, he wasn't feeling his bruises. His blood was running suddenly strong in his veins. The three troopers were edging forward, listening. McGaughey clenched his fists and his lips went hard. He had a debt to settle with these devils, and he intended to square the score at the earliest moment.

The trooper clerk ran his finger down the list. Turned a page and frowned and went on searching.

McGaughey said, softly, 'Try Erlington County.'

The lieutenant was startled. 'But that's clear across the state.'

Grey eyes met the lieutenant's. 'Anywhere in the state,' McGaughey quoted. 'That's what the draft summons said. Okay, here I am, reporting in Gin County.'

A voice behind them said, 'Don't sound so insolent, man.'

McGaughey turned. A cavalry captain was sitting on a window ledge, flicking flies with a hunting switch. A big, untidy man, careless about his unbuttoned tunic, with a lot of untidy hair sticking from under his cap and from all over his face. A bad-tempered-looking officer, with heavy eyes that looked over puffy flesh at a world in which only alcohol was solace.

The clerk had found the name under Erlington County. He read out 'McGaughey, James Clarke, twenty-eight, bachelor.' Then stopped.

The bored lieutenant called impatiently, 'Go on, man.' At the next table the man pleased because he had lost two fingers walked across to the surgeon, displayed his maimed hand for a second and then went out into the world a free man again. On his right another lieutenant was getting angry with a particularly stupid draftee who couldn't answer simple questions.

The clerk said, puzzled, 'Occupation — *doctor*.'

'Doctor!'

The surgeon over by the door let his chair drop on all four legs.

'You a doctor?' The lieutenant hadn't met one on a draft before. He tried to feel his way carefully. McGaughey nodded. The heavy captain was slouching across. Only the lieutenant at the next table, repeating a question for the third time, wasn't interested in the drama at that centre table.

'Doctors don't need to go on the draft.' The lieutenant was puzzled. If a doctor wasn't in the army, with a good paid post as surgeon, he could find many ways of lining his pocket with this war on. Like those quacks outside.

McGaughey shrugged. 'I never asked for exemption.' That was as much as he wanted to say.

There was a stillness in the room. It lasted for only a brief second, and yet it showed how all interest was upon him . . . a doctor electing to join the army as a common trooper.

The 'common troopers' at the door

stared at him as if he were crazy. The three troopers together watched him as if withdrawn into themselves, heads down, suspicion in those eyes peering under ragged eyebrows.

The big, coarse-looking captain, loose tunic swinging open to show an unfastened blue shirt and hairy chest, stood so close to McGaughey he was almost touching him. His eyes seemed to hold a perpetual look of anger; they peered over the puffy folds of flesh as if annoyed that a man should claim to be a doctor.

'A doctor?' The captain's angry voice. 'Who says you're a doctor? Any fellar c'n buy a sheepskin an' set up his shingle in this state. That don't make a doctor.'

'Harvard says I'm a doctor.' McGaughey's voice was quite cool. He gave back look for look with that top-heavy captain. The lieutenant at the next table was shouting, 'Don't go to sleep on me!'

The captain jerked his head. 'Ned!'

The surgeon did not move for a second, then his head lifted and slowly he pulled himself off his chair. He was a shambles of a man, McGaughey thought. Untidier than the captain, just as big, perhaps softer in the flesh. Moustached like the captain, too, only his was grey and as ragged as a worn-out broom.

McGaughey's eyes narrowed. There was a resemblance between captain and surgeon. Only, the surgeon was much the older of the two. His glance took in the snuff stains on that surgeon's faded tunic.

'Ned, this fellar calls himself a doctor. Says he's been to Harvard. What have you got to say about that?'

The captain's small, brown, unpleasant eyes were on McGaughey while he spoke. The Harvard man had an impression that the captain was dictating the answer he wished to receive. His eyes switched back to the surgeon.

The regimental medical officer was listening in the manner of a man trying to focus upon words. He had a dull expression in his eyes that looked rather prominent, hard as marbles, perpetually staring. Looking at that empty face and sagging body McGaughey had a feeling of a man going to decay . . .

The surgeon's voice, as uncertain and untidy as he said, 'Harvard. School stuff. Don't learn nothin' from professors. That don't make him a doctor.' His hand fumbled inside his breast pocket for a tarnished, worn snuff box. He didn't fasten the pocket button when he replaced the tin.

The room shook as someone fell on to the dirty floorboards. Dust rose and danced in a myriad of bright lights. Startled faces were turned towards the end table. The younger man was out on the floor.

The lieutenants were on their feet behind the tables, their eyes quickly glancing towards the big captain, waiting for a lead. The captain stooped angrily, dragged the unconscious man half over on to his back until he had seen his face and then dropped him.

'Get him to his feet,' he shouted. 'Shamming sick won't keep him out of the army.' He began to swear under his breath, as if deliberately fomenting the ever-present anger within him.

Obedient troopers leapt to obey the command. There were three of them. They were rough in the way they dragged the youth in that grey shirt upright. Deliberately rough, as if by past experience knowing that that would find favour with their captain.

The youth's head was lolling. His dark hair was down across his face. But he made an effort to stand on his feet, a degree of consciousness returning with that sudden movement.

The captain seemed enraged because the youth didn't immediately stand upright without support. He shouted, 'Run him up and down the room. Let him see he can't pull the wool over our eyes.'

McGaughey glanced towards the regimental surgeon. The older, untidier man was just watching. There was no expression on his face.

The three troopers began to shake the youth; on their own account began to shout at him . . .

McGaughey caught one by the neck. It was a painful grip and the man howled, almost screamed. To the best of McGaughey's knowledge this was the trooper who had crippled him with that first treacherous kick. He let it hurt. The trooper released his hold on the youth and fell away.

McGaughey saw two blue-chinned, astonished faces. He shoved his hand into one of the faces and it staggered away. Then he caught hold of the sagging form and supported the youth unaided.

Again there was a second's astonished silence in that room. Officers, sergeant and troopers just looked at him. McGaughey let the youth sink into a chair. He was expecting trouble now.

But he said, calmly surveying them, 'We're not in the army yet. You can leave that rough stuff until we've signed the declaration. Meanwhile, this man is sick and needs attention, and that doesn't mean running him around a room!'

The captain's fury went up like a rocket. 'Arrest that man! He struck a serving soldier. Sergeant, take him under close arrest — '

The sergeant came jumping forward. He was an office-worker, and this wasn't the kind of task he wanted, but he had to obey orders. He was shouting to the troopers to seize McGaughey. Blue-shirted cavalrymen were leaping forward. The room shook to the tread of their heavy boots. They had never known such an incident before at an enrolment.

McGaughey, crouching, stepping back towards a wall, saw a brutal-faced trooper swinging in at him with a big, bunched fist. The trooper whose neck he had gripped so painfully.

That was how those troopers interpreted the order to seize him. They were going to rough him up in the process. That would please their captain, they knew.

McGaughey grew reckless. He wasn't the kind of man to take a thrashing unnecessarily. All right, he thought grimly, if they wanted a fight, he would give them one!

He leapt to meet the trooper. There was still a pain in his groin from that kick down on the wharf. At least he would get his own back now, he thought.

His fist beat the trooper to the punch. A nose flattened. Blood squirted. A man sick with pain went staggering out of the fight. The captain and the sergeant were shouting furiously. Not-so-eager troopers came battling in.

McGaughey was shouting insults, throwing discretion completely to the winds. He went jumping in at the men, driving them back with the fury of his attack. But they got him, dragged him into the middle of the room. Held his arms while someone battered away at his head. He had a glimpse through blood that came into his eyes of someone being carried quickly out through the far door.

A limp figure supported by two blue-chinned troopers.

A man incensed by the untoward activities came dragging McGaughey's assailant away. A lieutenant, the one who had given the fingerless draftee his exemption.

He was shouting, 'Stop this brawling immediately. Get back, all of you!'

McGaughey was allowed to reel away, blood pouring down his face. He heard a door open, a man shouted, 'He was foxin'! When we took him outside he ran away!'

McGaughey wiped away the blood. Saw one of his former assailants in the doorway. There was triumph on those brutal, blotched features. Then the eyes came to rest on McGaughey and there was suddenly speculation in them.

3

Trooper James Clarke McGaughey rode from the small-arms range with the rest of his company. Some of the men were singing a Union marching song, and McGaughey nearly joined in because the pains were right out of his body now, it was a glorious day, and he felt satisfied with the life.

He was satisfied even though he had joined the cavalry under circumstances which made him a marked man to authority and he would be without privileges for his first three months. That meant little to McGaughey. Their drills would be through in a fortnight, and then they could expect to be rushed down to Virginia where the battle still raged outside Richmond. No one could expect privileges there.

Ahead of them were the severe wood buildings of Gin County barracks. They were on top of a bare rise that came shouldering out of the sluggish brown Gin River. He saw the flag flying, heard buglers practising. Men were moving in formation on the big parade ground. Practising a ceremonial to delight the colonel's ladies when they should have been doing sabre practice, he thought ironically.

A side-spring buggy drawn by an old bone-bag of a horse was being pulled to one side ahead of them, where grassy banks, bleaching under the hot Iowa sun, narrowed the trail. The company began to ride past.

McGaughey was thinking idly of the enemies he had made, the three blue-chinned troopers who had assaulted him on the wharf. He had seen them occasionally around the barracks, but they weren't in his company and with six hundred men in the regiment it wasn't surprising that he saw them so little.

He was thinking, 'I'm fit now. There's a lot I want to know, a few scores I'm going to pay off.' He would begin to hunt for the troopers, would try to get them one by one. But they would be treacherous, he thought. They'd draw a gun or a knife on him sure as shot if they were cornered . . .

McGaughey was level with the buggy. The driver was keeping a willing, drooping horse at a standstill. McGaughey's startled eyes saw brown hair, brown unhappy eyes. Blue and red on a dress that looked less gay, in keeping with its mistress's subdued mood.

He was riding near to the back of the column. Watching the sergeant riding flank on them, he pulled out of line. 'My gal,' he kept muttering, watching ahead. His comrades responded by closing up, leaving him behind. He didn't dismount, just jockeyed so that he sat level with the girl on her high seat.

Saluting, McGaughey smiled. 'Now I'm a darned sojer, see?'

She smiled, uncertainly but still a smile. She had recognised him immediately. Her eyes seemed to be moving across his face and beyond him, never still, anxious, troubled.

He said, 'I thought you might want to see me.' But what he really meant was that he wanted to speak with her. There was much he wanted to know.

But she asked the questions. 'My brother — ' His thoughts flew immediately to that youth with the bruised face. Of course he would be her brother. 'Where is he, do you know?' Her voice was desperate, her eyes hot with anxiety.

'Your brother?' McGaughey tried to think. The last time he had seen the boy he had not been too clear in his head, didn't quite know what was happening.

'I can't find him!' He detected the rising note of panic in her voice. Watching that young face he saw how near she was to the tears of frantic desperation. 'He's not with the regiment!'

The company had halted, a couple of hundred yards up the track. The sergeant flanking the double column was looking back.

'He ran away from the Enrolment Office.' McGaughey was trying to see the picture of that moment clearly, but it was all too hazy. He stopped, remembering that brutal face that had announced the news from the doorway. Faintly remembered the cunning and triumph on it. He rubbed his chin reflectively. The sergeant and two men were galloping towards him.

'He couldn't have run away.' That desperate voice, certain, making him think back. 'I had to help him to the Council Building. It was his day to enrol. But he was made too ill by that cowardly attack to do any running. Besides, he was wanting to join; he wouldn't have run away. Not after what people said about the family.'

'No.' He had thought a little about this very subject a few times in the past busy days, but he had been too busy looking after himself to become greatly concerned by anyone else. 'He didn't seem well enough to do any running.'

Stones were kicking up under the

flying hooves as the three horsemen came down at a flat gallop. Dust rose and made hazy the bare huts on top of the hill.

The girl threw in another remark. 'He would have come back home to see me if he had run away. He wouldn't have left me worrying without any word of his safety, I know. Not Frank.'

'And you've heard nothing about him?'

She was leaning forward to talk above the drumming of those hooves. Tears of anxiety were filling those bright eyes. She shook her head. 'Today I heard there was a warrant for his arrest for failing to stand for examination. That was the first I knew. I came out to the barracks. No one knows anything about him.' She wrung her hands in anguish.

The sergeant and two cavalrymen were wheeling round him, dragging their horses to an abrupt halt. The troopers impassive, not unfriendly; the sergeant bouncing with rage in his saddle.

McGaughey looked at the man. The thin, pettish face seemed to leer at him because of a growth on the sergeant's right eyelid. Coldly McGaughey said, 'Sergeant, that's a cyst on your right eyelid. Soon it will have grown so big you won't be able to see out of that eye. Better get it cut out.'

Then he resumed his conversation with the girl as if his comrades had departed.

The troopers looked quickly at each other, wanting to grin. This was a cool one. The sergeant sat on his horse as thunderstruck. His lips moved, but no sound came from them. Then his fingers strayed up to that eyelid.

McGaughey was saying, 'I'll look for him. I think I know where I can get a lead.' Those blue-chinned troopers . . . 'Where do you live? I'll get word to you.'

'Who told you to drop out? I nearly reported in without you!' The sergeant's voice was almost a howl. If he had gone in without Trooper McGaughey, this cool-speaking trooper who had enlisted under such unusual circumstances . . .

'There's a cottage past the Butte's Fork on the south road out. It's the first one on the river side. We . . . live there.' Her voice wasn't panicky, near to hysteria any longer. That decisiveness in McGaughey's voice, his certainly about getting news of her brother, was calming, reassuring. Those eyes looked at him without fright in them now, filled only with eagerness.

The sergeant found his voice. 'Come on. Git movin'!' Anxiously he peered under that heavy lid to where the rest of the troop waited outside the barrack gates. There could be a lot of trouble for him after this, darn this new trooper.

McGaughey said, 'I'm coming.' Wheeled his horse, saluted the girl and said, 'I'll be along. Don't worry.'

Then, choosing his own pace and that not too fast, he began to canter along the trail. He certainly would be seeing her. He wanted to know what this deadly hostility was between her family and those three brutal-faced troopers. If the sergeant hadn't returned he would have asked her.

The sergeant galloped alongside, anxious to rejoin the waiting column. 'You won't be goin' into town, McGaughey,' he shouted. 'There's no leave for you this side of fall, the captain says.'

McGaughey looked at him. A smile came to his lips. He looked very cool, very confident, nearly arrogant, intimidating somehow to the rough sergeant.

'I'll be going to see my gal,' he said. 'You see if I don't, sarge!'

One of the troopers began to laugh. The sergeant glared and then went bolting to restart his troop. Some other horsemen were riding rapidly across the dusty plains to their west. It wouldn't do to be blocking the gate when they arrived.

McGaughey and the other two tropers fell in at the rear of the column. They began to ride through the broad gateway. One of the troopers grinned at

McGaughey and said, 'You for Richmond, brother. First draft out, you'll be in it!'

McGaughey's eyes twinkled but he said nothing. They were paraded, dismissed. Rode round to the stables, noisy with the sound of six hundred horses, and began to unsaddle.

While they were there, the other party of horsemen came wearily in. They were a detail from the reservations, come in for relief. They didn't look pleased with life.

Around the barracks that evening the talk was of the unrest in the reserves. This civil war had made men in high places forget their promises to the Sioux, and for half a year now they had received no food and none of the bounty that should have come to them. The Indians were starving, were making night forays on surrounding farms. No one had been killed yet, but the few guards on the reserve knew it would come. The Sioux would break out on the rampage again, the returning troopers swore.

'Me for Richmond,' a cavalryman said swilling coffee in the mess hut. 'I sure would rather fight Johnny Reb any day than them damned Sioux.'

McGaughey went out looking for the three troopers as soon as it was dark. They could tell him what had happened to that boy. He shivered. He wasn't so sure that he wanted to know. But for that girl's sake . . .

The lamps were lit in the huts, and the Post looked cheerful in the warm evening's darkness. In the sutler's hut there was singing, as troops thirsty from the day's drills got outside as much liquor as their pockets would afford. In the married quarters a baby was crying, and a laundress was nagging at an unseen soldier-husband. A piano played from the colonel's house, facing down the line of huts; a woman sang, followed by the sycophantic applause of the subalterns.

He crossed a patch of lamplight, heading towards the colonel's house.

RHQ lines were at that end. The three troopers had been in town on each of the enrolment days, therefore they would be headquarters' staff. If he hung around long enough he would spot them, he was sure.

He found the four huts that housed headquarters' troopers. A tree, planted for the delight of the colonel's pretty, doll-like wife, grew without enthusiasm in the sandy soil outside the huts. McGaughey leaned in the shadow against it. Stood there patiently and waited.

He wanted to meet them one at a time, because he was virtually without a weapon. From his leather case he had taken a surgeon's tool. It was a hollow needle, used for locating pockets of pus. That was his only defence. It was better than a knife, but he didn't intend to use it unless his own life was threatened.

His eyes watched the lamplit windows. Every few minutes a door opened, yellow oil light streamed out into the night. McGaughey grew rigid trying to recognise the figure entering or leaving the hut.

It was going to be difficult. He listened to the noise of men stamping within their barrack rooms, heard singing. Thought more than once he recognised a voice . . .

A man was sidling crab-like towards him from the shadows. His head was forward like a turtle's, peering, questing into the gloom. He was taking a few paces then halting. Moving another few yards and peering.

McGaughey watched him, rigid. Someone had spotted him walking across to that tree. Now he couldn't walk away because he would be seen, away from the tree's shadow. He crouched, waiting for the figure to approach.

It was starlight, surprisingly light now that his eyes were used to the night. But he couldn't recognise that silent, gliding, approaching figure.

Then a voice came. 'McGaughey.'

Sergeant Gehler.

McGaughey sighed and walked out into the open. 'Yeah?'

The sergeant came up. McGaughey could almost see him peering under that heavy eyelid at him. Gehler seemed suspicious. 'What are you doing, standing under a tree so long? What are you up to?'

McGaughey said, 'That's what the tree was put there for, wasn't it? For us to stand agen.'

Gehler hesitated. At normal times he would have been abrupt about that answer, but just then there was something else on his mind. A door swung open. Light streamed. Someone said something about getting a drink. The door slammed again.

McGaughey's pulse quickened. That voice and that form. He knew them. And just one of them. This was what he had been waiting for, but now Gehler was hanging on to his arm. He couldn't follow. Heard the heavy footsteps tramp away in the darkness.

Gehler was saying, 'Is that right what

you said about my eye? I don't want to be half-blind for the rest of my life.' He was a worried man.

McGaughey was cursing him, was wanting to go after that trooper. A man was riding in through the gateway fast. Gehler was holding him, his manner urgent.

'What can I do about it? They're saying you're a doctor. Are you?'

McGaughey said, resignedly, 'I won't deny it.' He relaxed. He'd forget about that trooper for a while. It was just bad luck the sergeant had spotted him and followed him. There'd be another time.

He said, 'This is a job for a surgeon. You go see him. If he knows his job it won't take more than a few minutes, won't hardly hurt at all.'

He wanted to get rid of him, but Gehler's voice came in an expressive explosion of disgust from the darkness — 'Him! He's a butcher. Nobody ever goes sick in this outfit. They daren't!'

'So?' McGaughey knew what was coming.

'I don't want to go blind in one eye.' That worried reiteration. 'You look as if you might be a good doctor. Can you do it?'

'You're asking me to break army rules. I'll be flogged on a wheel if the surgeon knows I've done his job for him.' That captain would see to that. He watched over his elder brother's interests like a jealous nannie, protecting him, prompting him, demanding respect for him. A queer pair, those officers.

The sergeant was desperate. 'No one will ever know. I'll see you're all right. I'll get you into town to see that gal of yours.'

'All right. Tomorrow.'

Light swung in a broad yellow beam from the company's office. A voice bellowed — 'Sergeant Gehler!' It was the duty officer.

Gehler swung round as if he had been shot. For a second he hesitated, repeated, 'Tomorrow.' And then went running across the parade ground.

McGaughey followed, simply because the trooper had also gone the same way.

There was a commotion outside the company office. He could see the sergeant standing stiffly to attention just inside the open doorway, could hear the lieutenant's voice. There was something about the scene that stirred curiosity. A few men, passing down the lines, lingered, trying to hear that voice. McGaughey came up behind them, but he was looking at faces, trying to spot his man.

Gehler saluted, turned about and ran down the three shallow steps on to the parade ground. He saw the men hesitating, beginning to sheer off. Called, 'Stand where you are. I want five men urgently. You, you — and you.'

McGaughey was among them. The sergeant must have seen his face, hesitated, then said, 'Not you.' And grabbed another drifter. McGaughey felt that he was securing a down payment of a favour in advance of tomorrow's operation.

The last man to be grabbed said angrily, 'What's it for? A dirty job? I always get dirty jobs. Why do I always have to be around when they come up?'

Gehler snapped, 'Shut that face and listen. There's a body got blown against the river bank downstream a quarter of a mile. It's got to be moved before the colonel's lady goes ridin' in the mornin'.'

McGaughey turned in the darkness. Gehler was giving orders. 'Get picket horses. Two of you bring the light ambulance. Oh, an' bring some old canvas and a bit of rope.'

McGaughey went back to the sergeant. 'I want to go out with this party, sarge.' He wanted to see that body, had a suspicion about it. Gehler hesitated. McGaughey said, 'Remember . . . tomorrow.'

Gehler snapped, 'You, Rosser, drop out. McGaughey, get your hoss.'

As the Harvard man turned he heard someone running across the parade ground, big boots making a heavy, thumping sound in the darkness. As he swung into the saddle of one of the picket horses, always ready for emergency use by the guard house, McGaughey looked back towards the headquarters' huts. A door was opening, light falling out. But it was too far for him to distinguish features.

They had to get a pair of mules into the shafts of the light, two-wheeled ambulance. They took objection to having their night's rest disturbed and kicked about. But in the end the little party took the river road.

McGaughey realised that Gehler was keeping very close to him. After a time he said, drily, 'You don't need to worry, sarge. I'll be around with my knife tomorrow.'

Gehler wasn't sure. Suspicion edged his voice in the darkness. 'Why should a feller volunteer to go collect a corpse? You ever seen a corpse that's bin fished out of the Gin?'

'I'm a doctor. I reckon I've seen my share of bodies.' I'm a doctor.

McGaughey left that as an explanation for volunteering. It seemed to satisfy Gehler.

He talked now, showing friendliness. 'Wonder who it is? Fellow who found it was a teamster bringin' in a tired hoss. It shied. That's what made him look. He don't like corpses, an' after that his hoss wasn't tired no more.'

'I heard it galloping in,' McGaughey said drily. He was listening. Someone else was riding the river trail. Someone had cut right across the grassland instead of following the bend as they had to do with the high-wheeled ambulance. Someone was ahead. It made McGaughey wonder.

They halted the ambulance, then all dismounted and began to search along the edge of the river. They searched for a good hour, and the moon came up to help them, but they never found a trace of a corpse. At length the sergeant called them together.

'Darn teamster,' a trooper was swearing. This was sleep they were missing. 'Bet there never was a corpse!'

Gehler was tired and fed up. 'If there was I reckon the current swung it back into midstream. He should have dragged it out of the water.'

McGaughey, mounting, was thinking, 'It could have been pushed back into the current.' Those hooves ahead of them along the trail as they came down from the Post . . .

He was making decisions. Gehler was saying from his saddle, 'Darn fool, whoever he was, goin' an' fallin' in the river. Or was it suicide?'

McGaughey's voice. 'I'll lay money on it, it was neither, sarge. My hunch is — it was murder!'

And his hunch gave him the identity of that drifting body out there in the slow stream.

4

Gehler repeated, 'Murder? What makes you think that? Don't you go sayin' murder up at the Post or we'll spend days hangin' round an enquiry room.'

McGaughey had made up his mind. He was riding his horse against Gehler's, was edging him away from the mules and the ambulance and the other weary troopers.

He leaned forward in his saddle, startling the sergeant with his demand. 'Sarge, I want you to detail me off to search the river bank as far as Gin Point.'

Gehler got it. 'You want to visit that gal of yours!' He shook his head decidedly. 'Not on your life. You're confined to barracks for three months except when out on duty, remember.'

'This would be out on duty.' Again Gehler obstinately shook his head.

Temper flared in McGaughey. 'Then go blind, man, go blind! I won't touch that darned eye. Go let that old drunkard knife you instead!'

Gehler hesitated. McGaughey could see that heavy eyelid trying to lift the better for his two eyes to focus on the new trooper's face. Gehler sighed, tried to sound firm and authorative. 'Trooper McGaughey, ride down the bank another mile and see what you can find. Report to me on your return to barracks.'

They rode off with the trundling ambulance, Gehler a worried, unhappy man. McGaughey clapped heels into the sides of his horse and went racing through the night down the river road. He was going to see his 'gal.' Now he had to know what all this mystery was about, why it was necessary for a man to be killed to quieten him.

Murder. That was ugly. It couldn't be tolerated in a community; had to be punished. And he was sure that the girl's brother had been murdered, was that corpse out on the bosom of the sluggish Gin River right then.

Butte's Fork. South road out, first cottage on the river side. It was there, small, huddling in among silent elms, no light in its tiny windows. The nearest neighbour was a hundred yards along the rutted track. It was no place for a girl to live on her own, he thought, halting his horse in some shadows down the road. If she lived alone, that was.

The moon, rising now and very bright, poured whiteness upon the scene, touching the shingles and intensifying the black shadows around the porch. Brooding, hating what he had to do, McGaughey had a feeling of unrest, an inward indecision that was unease if it was not fear.

Everything was too still. There was something malignant about the night's unmoving silence, a sense of something watching, waiting. Or did it remind him of death?

He moved at length towards a small

gate that stood between high overgrown hedges, ragged thorns that stretched out in the night and plucked on his sleeve as he dismounted. He drew away, shivering. His eyes went around, looked everywhere into pools of intense blackness that could have hidden a regiment of lurking men.

He felt naked, exposed, standing there beside his horse, head bent forward and peering. But he had to go in.

There was a short hitching bar to the left of the gate. He tied his mount to it and lifted the latch. The hinges creaked, a long-drawn, agonising note. It brought him to a halt, his head twisting to look at the nearest shadows. His back shivered, turned once more to the darkness.

'Darn it, and you a doctor!' McGaughey thought. He had never felt like this before, for a moment couldn't understand it now. Then he decided it was because never before had he felt his life in danger from a nightly visit to someone's cottage.

Never? That wasn't quite true . . .

Gently he tapped on the door. It wouldn't be good for the girl if neighbours saw a trooper knocking on her door at midnight. Once again he tapped, watching around him, across the tiny herb garden that was sweet to his nostrils in the night's stillness, over that hedge that was as ragged as the regimental surgeon's moustache. Black and white, moonlight and shadows beyond. But nothing moving. Too still.

A voice whispered, 'Who's there?' Startling him. The girl's voice on the other side of that door.

He drew in a breath. Just as softly said, 'Me. You won't know my name. Jim McGaughey.'

But she knew his voice. 'You. Yes, I know you.' The door remained closed. 'What do you want?' There was fear in that soft voice.

'I want to speak to you. I told you I would come.'

Her voice, quick, suddenly eager,

hopeful. 'Frank! Is it about him? Is he all right?'

A pause. Fear gripped her. 'Something's happened to him.'

She forgot her fears. There was a fumbling, a bolt went back, a chain dropped. The door opened. He saw movement in the shadows, a white, staring face against the soft blackness.

She was coming out into the moonlight. McGaughey pushed her inside.

'Don't show yourself. Don't come outside.'

There was that fear on him again, that feeling that eyes watched. His scalp was moving, prickling, trying to erect itself like some primitive being. That darned moonlight. It was chilling, scaring . . . revealing.

His horse stamped, blew through soft, quivering nostrils, then tossed its head. He heard the jingle of bridle metal, wished he could bring his mount inside. But that wasn't possible.

He stepped over the threshold. The

girl gasped, alarmed. Then he hurriedly slammed the door and a cry came from unseen lips.

'Stop it,' he ordered, his tone peremartory, authorative. The tone his patients had been wont to obey. She obeyed. He ordered, 'If the shutters are up, light a lamp.'

He slipped a bolt across, heard the girl moving in the darkness. She was using a flint box. Matches were scarce among civilians, he thought. There were sparks, a glow. She was blowing. A flame, then the lamp was lit.

He turned as she set the lamp on the table. The yellow light threw shadows up her face, made her hair shine almost as if it were alight. She was watching him.

He looked at the window. It was shuttered, all right. But there were cracks to every shutter and he kept glancing window-wards throughout their conversation.

The room was small. It was kitchen, living room and parlour all in one. A steep flight of unrailed steps led to an upstairs room. There would be one bedroom above, he thought. All these cottages were the same, and he had sat in hundreds of them, sat and watched men, women and children grow well, grow ill . . . and die.

He pulled up a hardbacked chair to the bare, scrubbed-top table. There was little furniture in the room. Two more chairs. A sideboard, New England-like arrayed with crockery. A plank cupboard and a crude wooden chest. A cluster of pans around the dead fire completed the furnishings.

McGaughey smiled reassuringly. 'Sit down,' he murmured. 'You don't need to fear me.' His glance went towards the shuttered window. 'I'm jumpy tonight, but I guess that's no reason why you should feel afraid.'

'Jumpy?' Those big eyes leapt towards the shuttered window. 'Why? Is there someone . . . outside?'

'I don't know.' He shrugged. 'I'm an old woman, I reckon, getting scared of a few shadows.' But shadows could contain guns, and he was sure he knew men who had killed and might feel they had to kill again. 'I got a feeling I was being watched outside. Nothing to go on, but — well, I had that feeling.'

She was afraid again, but not now of him. He saw her eyes go again quickly towards that shuttered window; then she sat down on a chair drawn to the table, crouched across it, as if being close to McGaughey would be protection. Her face didn't turn away from that silent, reflecting, small-paned window.

McGaughey reached across and took her hands in his. He spoke cheerfully, wanting to comfort her, because there were worse things she had to know.

'There's nothing to fear now. The door's locked, those shutters look strong enough. We're safe inside.'

He felt her relax. Her head came round. Her face was close to his. Her lips parted and he caught the bright gleam of lamplight on white, even teeth.

'I'm terrified. I want to go back to the town.' She shuddered and her eyes partly closed as if to shut out a nightmare. 'I — I lie awake and hear noises and imagine things — '

She stopped. He felt her grip his hands. Somewhere wood was scraping, scratching.

McGaughey said, 'Mice,' and again she relaxed. The scraping stopped, small feet scurried away.

'But they don't always sound like mice, those noises.' She had lifted her face to his again, seemed to be pleading to be believed. 'I shouldn't have stayed here when Frank . . . went.'

McGaughey said, 'You mustn't stay here. We'll find another place for you.' He had been thinking about that ever since he had seen for the first time the loneliness of this tiny, riverside cottage. It was no place for a girl, this girl. He had a feeling that somewhere men were panic-stricken and desperate; that it was to be this girl's turn next.

'No, you can't stay here.'

* * *

His head jerked towards the door. Outside, his horse blew again through tremulous nostrils. There was the jingle of bridle metal. He wondered, 'Is there someone out there disturbing him . . . '

The girl spoke. Her eyes seemed bigger than ever in that lamplight. 'Frank.' Her brother. 'What do you know of him?'

He was a man experienced in breaking bad news. He never liked it, liked doing it still less now with those frightened, beseeching eyes upon him.

His grip tightened on her strong hands. 'I've no certain information. But I don't think you'd be without news from your brother now if he were — '

'Alive.' She finished the sentence. She was shocked. Her face contorted and she rocked in her agony.

He wouldn't tell her about the reported body in the river. I've nothing to go on,' he repeated. 'But I think you should be prepared for the worst. I came to you tonight because I think you are in danger yourself. And I want to know what it is at the back of all this mystery.'

She could only look at him, and now tears brimmed into her eyes, sparkling bright in the steady flame from the lamp between them. Lovely eyes. His pulse stirred. He knew then that he wanted this girl.

She screamed, a quick, stifled inhalation, her head twisting, eyes following some slight sound to the door. The latch was raised. It dropped, the noise of metal on metal lost in the tail of her scream.

McGaughey lifted, reared over the lamp and blew. They were in darkness. The girl was round the table in an instant, clinging to him, her breath sobbing. McGaughey held her, trying with his strength to bring comfort to the shaking body.

'Someone's outside,' she whispered.

'But I'm here; the door's locked and the shutters look good.' He had a weapon, too, for close quarters, he remembered; that hollow needle from his surgical roll. His teeth set in the darkness. He felt jumpy, nervy, too. But just let anyone try to get in this house this night.

There was no sound outside. Then the girl said, her voice as soft as a night breeze, 'I heard it earlier, that latch. Or I thought I did. It was just before you came.'

Now he remembered she was dressed; he hadn't thought to be curious about it before. But if she had been disturbed earlier . . .

She had to know the truth. Innocence was no protection where killers were concerned. 'You're in danger. I'm sure of it. Not just ordinary danger from men, either. I want to know why. Why are men wanting to harm you? Why did they — ' he nearly said, 'kill your brother?' Then changed it to — 'fear your brother?'

'Fear?' She stirred against his chest. There was no sound from outside, but both were listening. 'No one could have feared Frank. There was nothing to fear about him. I — I don't understand — anything.'

She was tired, overwrought, suddenly weak. He held her close again to him and stroked her shoulder, so warm to his touch under her thin cotton dress. When she moved, her hair caressed his face and left it tingling from the touch.

He said, 'I think they've gone. Perhaps your scream scared 'em.' Maybe they had hoped to surprise them, but now realised there could be no surprise. And they wouldn't know he was unarmed but for that probe.

'There's no gun in the house?' She shook her head. 'We'll wait a while, then we'll go.'

They stood and listened. The mouse was busy again, and the sound of its gnawing little teeth seemed to fill the house. Their ears ignored it, listened for other sounds outside. McGaughey's horse was restless and kept moving. But it was still there, and that was a good thing. The moon must have cleared some trees and a pencil of white light stole where the shutters failed to meet. It searched across the room, widening on the table, touching the dead oil lamp with whiteness.

But nothing in the next half hour came to interrupt that beam.

McGaughey said, 'Now think. Why do men fear you? Why must you be silenced?' Men. Those troopers, of course. Three suddenly frightened men acting desperately, even cautiously, fear driving them. Fear? Always that word. Then it was fear for their own skins, for their necks, if they were prepared to kill this girl, as he was sure they intended.

She said, 'It must be a mistake. There is no reason why anyone should fear me.' She was trembling again, bewildered to feel herself the centre of a pattern of violence.

Patiently he tried again. All the time he was listening standing there in the darkness, his eyes on that slowly moving shaft of moonlight that never for an instant was blocked by a bulky, crouching form beyond the shutters.

'That day last week when you were in Gin Point. What happened? You were with your brother.'

'We were in for the enrolment. Frank was up for the draft for the army.'

'And he was looking forward to it, wanted to join?'

'Yes. He was an Abolitionist. Besides, it was adventure. He wanted to be in uniform, riding a fine horse. He was young and saw war as an exhilarating cavalry charge.'

Softly — 'But you don't see it that way?'

'No.' A sigh. 'I saw only the loneliness. First my father, then Frank gone. And Frank would be in danger all the time.' She stirred against his chest. 'I've seen fine men leave this town, proud of themselves, sure nothing would happen to them. And I've seen them return, without legs, without arms, without eyes. Men ruined by the war. I didn't want to see Frank like that

— or not return at all.'

'What happened, on Main Street?'

Her voice was bewildered. 'I don't know. Frank was by my side, holding my arm. We were coming down to the river to the Council Buildings. I wasn't looking at him.'

McGaughey felt that sudden racing of his pulse again. He wanted to ask whom she was looking at, but didn't dare.

'He just let go of my arm. When I turned my head he was standing in the street, saying something to three cavalrymen. The middle one immediately struck him.' He felt her body shudder within his arms. 'It was a swift, savage blow. A — a murderous blow, and I don't know why. Frank wasn't ready for it and he went down.'

'It was a hard blow. Frank . . . your brother . . . was still dazed by it hours later. Perhaps he hurt his head, too, when he fell to the ground.'

'They were drunk, of course. Some of these troopers are bad, brutal men.

But — but I still can't understand why they should strike poor Frank. I'm sure he didn't even know them.'

He remembered her words down on the wharf. 'You said you thought I was going to interfere?'

'I thought so.' Her voice murmuring up from his chest. 'When I looked back at you, you seemed about to jump at the trooper. But you didn't.'

'It's a wise man that keeps out of drunken brawls,' he defended. His heart was thumping pleasurably. Back, she had said. She had been looking at him before the incident. His tongue seemed clumsy, but he had to follow the opening. 'Why were you looking at me in the first place?'

She was suddenly shy. Suddenly felt conscious of her position there in his arms in the darkness. She murmured, 'I — I don't know,' and tried to withdraw from his embrace. Purposely he held her and she relaxed and stood submissively as before.

'And you have no idea why your

brother should leave you to speak to those troopers, why he should be struck down for what he said?'

'No. No idea.'

McGaughey sighed. He was thinking, 'It's time to go.' He couldn't stay here all night. That would mean trouble for him — and for Sergeant Gehler. Poor Gehler was probably not sleeping right now.

'Get a cloak,' he ordered. 'You can't stay here alone.'

'Where are you taking me?' She had moved away, was over by the door. He felt a draught as she swung a dark cloak.

'Back to camp. You'll be all right.' Safer right under the noses of those three murderous troopers than here he thought. He'd be able to look after her.

Then he went to open the door.

5

His horse, curiously white in that moonlight, pricked up its ears and stared at him as he stood inside the shadowy porch. It dragged an impatient paw and made snuffling, horsey sounds.

McGaughey listened, listened beyond those familiar sounds: and heard nothing. His eyes probed the shadowy hollows of the hillside, the gloom where trees threw deep shadows. Just whiteness, shadows and stillness. Nothing to be seen, everything to fear.

The girl was behind him. He felt the stir of her cloak against his back. She would be nervous, her heart racing wildly, he knew. His hand reached back. She put hers in his.

Swiftly they went down to the gate, keeping to the shadows of the hedge. Pausing, he looked along the track. His nerves were tense. It didn't seem possible that their enemies would have gone.

But they had. He unhitched his horse, lifted the girl into the saddle and swung up. They rode quickly away up river, and no one tried to stop them.

'That scream must have scared 'em out of the county,' he said at length.

'So we needn't have stood there in the cottage all that while.'

'No.' But he was glad they had. Glad that still she was soft and warm within his arms.

'You've no relations? Or friends?' She shook her head. He remembered her father; she had mentioned him. 'What happened to your father?'

'He's dead.' He had guessed that. 'It happened less than two months ago.' Her voice stopped, as if her thoughts were suddenly choking her.

'What happened?' They were galloping steadily along the moonlit river trail. Her face was white in the brilliant moonlight, white and beautiful and so near to his own he wanted to kiss her.

She turned her head from him, gazed up the winding trail.

'He was killed. We found him, Frank and I. They — they had hanged him. Poor dad!'

She began to cry, to weep out the agony, the anguish of those past weeks. Wept against his chest while he stroked her hair and tried to comfort her. They were near to the barracks when at last she recovered some of her composure. For the moment he avoided speaking about her father.

'It doesn't seem more than a few minutes since I was on this trail before. I — I'm glad I came.' She wasn't looking at him. He knew what she meant. She was glad she had met him again. A sentry had moved into the roadway by the guardhouse.

McGaughey suddenly snapped his fingers. Why hadn't he thought of it before! That had been faintly puzzling him — why her enemies had come after her this night and not earlier.

Because that day she had driven out

to the barracks. She had been seen. The three troopers must have seen her and must have thought she represented danger.

It was puzzling, all very mysterious. But he felt that in the end it would all add up. The one thing was, for the moment the girl was safe . . .

The sentry challenged them, bellowing suddenly at the top of his voice just to show he was wide awake. The horse took fright and tried to sidle away. McGaughey fought to get it under control and edged in near to the lamp over the guardhouse. A huddled figure in a long coat glowered behind a rigid rifle at them.

McGaughey said, 'Man, stop playing soldiers. Sergeant Gehler told you I'd be riding in soon, didn't he? Then why waken the camp?'

The tone made the sentry shuffle his feet. Then indignation asserted itself. 'Don't talk so high an' mighty, soldier.' His rifle prodded unpleasantly. 'And don't bring that gal in here.'

'Why not?' McGaughey's tone was pleasant. Someone was walking into the lamplight, someone who couldn't sleep. 'She's a laundress. I found her back on the road. She'd stopped in town too long, I reckon.' Then he added: 'Been drinking, I guess.'

The girl stiffened, then relaxed, perhaps detecting what was not obvious to the affronted sentry, a note of humour in his voice.

'A laundress?' The sentry peered. 'I never saw her afore.'

Sergeant Gehler was standing there, his head tilted so that he could see under that drooping eyelid. There was relief on his thin face. He had been worrying.

'What's your report, soldier? Did you see that body anywhere?' The sergeant was very military before that sentry.

The girl was listening, perhaps suspecting. McGaughey saw her hands clench along the edge of her cloak.

The trooper's voice was formal. 'Nothing, sergeant. I never saw anything.'

He was riding his horse past the sentry. The man had grounded his gun, was looking perplexed. Then he shrugged. The sergeant had seemingly accepted responsibility. He went back to his corner.

McGaughey began to move towards the married quarters. Gehler walked by his stirrup, lifting his thin face to say, 'You took a long time. What were you doing?' His eyes were suspicious, resting on the girl. 'Is she a laundress?'

McGaughey just laughed. He set his horse into a canter, so that the sergeant fell behind. Gehler called on the trooper to stop, but he didn't dare lift his voice. McGaughey rode on, leaving a fuming, uncertain, frustrated cavalry sergeant standing on the moon-swept parade ground.

The married quarters, close by the river, were not yet all occupied, the regiment being in the process of establishment. McGaughey put the girl inside an untenanted house. There was a bed and he brought blankets — his own, but he didn't tell her. Because there was no key he showed her how to wedge a chair against the door so that it was impossible for anyone to force their way in.

'Sleep well,' he advised. 'You're safe here. Tomorrow, make yourself a real laundress. Find some motherly soul and tack yourself on to her. No one will know any the better for some days, and by then we'll know what to do with you.'

She was smiling when he left her. She was grateful; there was a warmth in her eyes that made him dance in his stride as he walked his tired mount across to the stables. Then his smile faded. He realised he didn't even know her name.

* * *

Sergeant Gehler was apprehensive, nervously following the confident humming McGaughey into the rough ground north of the camp. An operation, especially so near to the eye, was something to be feared, but on top of that, if he were discovered submitting to surgery at the hands of other than the regimental surgeon —

He shuddered. But the prospect of blindness, even in one eye only, drove him to accept the situation. For some time he had been worrying about that increasing heaviness of his eyelid, had been wretchedly sure that soon he would be discharged the service because of a deficiency in vision.

McGaughey ordered, 'Lie down.' His glance had assured him that here they were safe. No one ever came this way, into the rough ground; there was no reason for anyone to do so.

McGaughey unwrapped a leather surgical case and withdrew a fine, bright, needle-sharp lance. Gehler watched, fascinated. He felt reassured by those strong hands, those swift, certain movements.

'What are you doing as a trooper?' he growled as McGaughey bent over his head. McGaughey shrugged but didn't answer.

'Keep still,' he ordered instead, his

voice so authoritative that Gehler couldn't think to move afterwards. 'This is a very simple operation. If you don't move at the wrong moment it should all be over in less than two minutes and you won't feel much pain. I'll take it out from under your eyelid and then your pretty face won't show a scar.'

The sergeant flinched as practised fingers folded back the offending eyelid. He saw steel, felt sharp pain as the razor-point sliced open his skin. Liquid . . . perhaps it was blood . . . clouded his eye and he tried to blink but those firm fingers wouldn't let him. McGaughey was pulling something out with a small piece of white linen.

'It's finished,' he said abruptly, sitting back on his heels. The sergeant sat up slowly, holding his head down against the sharp pain in his eyelid. McGaughey smiled. 'It'll smart for a few hours, but it wasn't bad, was it?'

Gehler shook his head. 'If it's been done right — '

McGaughey put his lance away, rose to his feet. 'It's done all right. That won't bother you again. It'll be a bit mucky for the rest of the day, bleeding a little perhaps, but don't let that worry you. You'll find that eyelid just as good as ever it was.'

Gehler held a handkerchief to his eye. His thin face looked up at McGaughey's and there was gratefulness in it. 'I won't forget this, trooper. You see, I'll make it up to you.'

McGaughey laughed, clapping his hand on the man's shoulder. There was no deference to rank at that moment; if anything, it was the other way round.

'That's what they all say. But within a week they've usually forgotten all about it. Better do it quickly if you're going to do anything at all, sarge,' he joked.

They began to walk back towards the camp. Then both halted. Blue uniforms were across their path. Troopers. Three of them. McGaughey went rigid at the sight of them, his eyes alert for danger.

They were halted, almost crouching,

McGaughey thought, their heavy, blue-chinned faces warily watching. Wary, he realised, not threatening for the moment. Swiftly he thought. 'They saw me come this way, followed, maybe thinking to get me alone.'

Perhaps they hadn't expected to see him return so quickly in the company of the sergeant, and now they were disconcerted. Gehler bellowed, 'What in hell are you doing here? Get back to camp.' Though they had as much right there as anyone.

There was an edge of panic in the sergeant's voice, and he looked uneasily after the trio as they shambled away. 'D'you think they saw?' he whispered.

'No.' McGaughey shook his head. 'I don't think so.' Then he asked: 'You know them?'

'Them? Sure I know them.' They were going in towards the buildings. 'Headquarters' staff. Troopers Binney, Collet and Feiner.' Gehler was feeling easier now. 'Bad medicine, them fellers. They get in too much trouble. They drink too much. Don't know where they get their money from, but they've always plenty for booze, especially lately.'

He looked around. No one was in sight. Held out his hand and let his features relax into an unaccustomed smile. 'Thanks, trooper — again. You see, I'll make things all right for what you've done!'

'Good. That's what I like to hear.' McGaughey was hearty, smiling a large smile at the sergeant. 'I'm sure you'll be a power of help to me. To start with, you know that laundress that came in last night?'

The smile was going from Gehler's face. He held his handkerchief to his eye as if he were crying. 'What about her?'

'She's no laundress. She's . . . my gal. I'll be asking you to help her when I can think what to do.' McGaughey nodded pleasantly and went on to his barrack room. He had to get some blankets; last night had been cold without any.

Sergeant Gehler looked after him and there was no friendliness in his gaze. Perhaps he saw a nightmare time ahead for him, buying the silence of this confident easy-smiling trooper-surgeon; a never-ending demand for assistance that wouldn't be countenanced by a superior officer.

Perhaps that thought decided him . . . or perhaps he was really trying to help McGaughey stay alive. He went quickly down to the company office.

* * *

McGaughey had just bought some blankets from an old soldier who had more than he should have. He was watching a small parade of horsemen over by the company office, was wanting them to get out of the way so that he could go discreetly and look for the girl. He hadn't seen her since the previous night, but he wasn't worried on her behalf. In this busy place no one would question her right to be there, provided she did a share of laundering.

He saw Gehler, handkerchief held to his eye. He came out of the company office in a hurry and went as fast as his legs could go among the huts. Then McGaughey saw a runner from the company office. He had a piece of paper in his hand and was coming straight towards McGaughey's hut. McGaughey suddenly stood upright, his eyes narrowing. A premonition of trouble seized him.

When the runner kicked back the door McGaughey was facing him.

'Trooper McGaughey.'

The runner looked round. Men were sitting on their beds, getting ready for first parade. McGaughey went across.

'You McGaughey?' The Harvard man didn't like the way the runner pronounced his name. He called him M'Goy.

'M'Goffy,' he corrected.

'M'Goffy, then.' The runner spat his indifference to pronounciation out through the open doorway. 'You've got five minutes. Pack your kit, draw a hoss an' parade right sharp. Lootenant Alabastor doesn't like standing.'

'What?' Alarm widened McGaughey's eyes. 'Where d'you think I'm going?' But his heart was pounding. Right then he knew this was a clear upset to his plans.

The runner was going out. 'You're goin' to Injun country. There's a man got himself kicked by his horse. Got himself some ribs that rattle now, I guess. You're named for his place.'

'Why me?' McGaughey began to say, and then his eyes went over among the huts where he had last seen the sergeant with the sore eye. 'Gehler,' he whispered viciously to himself. 'You did this, darn you!'

Gehler was getting rid of him before he found McGaughey involving him in deep trouble. The way McGaughey did things was frightening to an orthodox army man.

'Doesn't like being blackmailed,' McGaughey thought, and it made him grin. But he was worried. There was no time for him to go and see the girl. She was being left inside the camp, all alone and defenceless. And she wouldn't even know he had left, would go on waiting for him to turn up, and he never would. He didn't know her name, couldn't send a note to her.

'Oh, blast!' he shouted angrily, and began to roll his kit in his newly-purchased blankets.

'What you swearin' for?' a stunted, depressed little trooper wanted to know. 'You're gettin' out of the war. You won't ever see Richmond, so I guess you'll go on stayin' alive.'

Most of the men there would gladly have changed places with him, though the previous night they'd been shaking their heads at the news from the Sioux reserves.

He ran for a horse, got one and came galloping up to the agency detail. Lieutenant Alabastor was the young lieutenant who had stopped the fighting in the Enrolment Office. He was a bit biting with his tongue, an impatient, quick-tempered man, but McGaughey thought he wasn't a bad officer.

He was shouting, 'Make it smarter next time, trooper, or you'll find your back to a cartwheel.' But that was all he said. A threat of punishment but no more than that.

Ten minutes later they had been inspected by their captain, that over-heavy, angry-faced officer, and were riding out. McGaughey was straining his eyes all the time trying to see the girl, hoping to catch her attention so that she would realise he was being detailed away from camp.

But she was nowhere in sight. He went out without seeing her, and was dejected and unhappy in consequence.

A side-spring buggy had pulled to one side, just beyond the guardhouse, to let the detail ride through. McGaughey had an impression of a big man sitting under a wide-brimmed straw hat, one thumb hooked into the armhole of his stained vest. He saw a heavy face that yet looked intelligent, a moustache that was big and brown-stained where it was not grey.

One of the detail exclaimed softly, 'The marshal. Someone else been troublin' the town!' By the sound of it, the marshal of Gin County was a fairly frequent visitor to the barracks.

But McGaughey paid little heed of the law. He was trying to sort out the mess he was in . . . the girl, rather, though he took responsibility for her plight. After a time he decided that as soon as they met anyone returning to the barracks he would send a letter by him to Sergeant Gehler. Gehler would know what he, McGaughey, thought of him; more, Gehler would be told to find the girl and see her to a place of safety.

He wrinkled his nose. So far as the girl was concerned, where was safety? He shelved the problem for the moment; a solution would come later, he thought optimistically. He was beginning to enjoy this ride.

And if Gehler thought to refuse? His

face smiled grimly. There would be a threat in that letter, he promised himself. If Gehler did not co-operate, someone might get to know about that unusual operation . . .

6

The Atchison Agency, to which they were reporting, was two days' ride away — longer if they met with bad weather. But the weather looked settled, too hot, if anything, and mostly much too dry.

On the first day they were in older, settled country, country which had long been cleared for farming. It was too open for them, and they sweated and their mouths grew caked and unpleasant as the dry dust rose under the hooves of their horses.

But towards nightfall they rode into wilder country, territory that had been ceded to the white man when the Sioux regretfully took to the reservations.

It was pleasantly wooded, so that they found good shade from the early summer sun, and their spirits rose as they relaxed under the spreading green branches. New settlements were appearing, however, and along the distant valleys they caught the ring of the woodman's axe as he cleared more land for planting.

They camped close against the land of a Dutch immigrant settler that night. There was no friendliness displayed towards the soldiers. There was a daughter of marriageable age in the Dutch family, and they were afraid for her with these rough soldiers about. McGaughey didn't blame them. He had no illusions about some of his companions.

'They'll be glad enough to see us if them blamed Sioux gets scalpin' ideas agen,' one of the troopers growled, a quick-eyed man who seemed furtively on the lookout for something all the while. He said something softly to a thin, silent comrade who was sucking a hollow tooth. Presently the pair went off to see what they could thieve in the way of food.

Their camp was pleasant — on a stretch of soft, close-cropped green grass bordering a winding, shingle-bedded stream of clear water. Fish darted away as they came to wash and bathe their hot feet. Rabbits scuttled among the thick foliage under the pressing wall of oaks and beeches.

When they had cooked and eaten their evening meal, the sun's still-warm rays upon them, they relaxed around the campfire. McGaughey was watching the thin spiral of smoke dissolving in the evening sky. Someone came and sat beside him.

It was Lieutenant Alabastor.

The lieutenant wanted companionship. His sergeant in charge of this detail was a rugged man with few ideas outside maintaining discipline. As a conversationalist, he was soon finished.

The lieutenant nodded to McGaughey. 'You can read?' Not all his men could, but he must have known McGaughey was a Harvard man — news like that soon got around — so his question could only have been an overture to conversation.

McGaughey nodded. He wanted to be alone with his thoughts. He was thinking that the girl might follow up after him into the territory. At the moment he was daydreaming, remembering her charm, the softness of her body, the warmth under his touch. He refused to face up to the implications of what he was thinking. For when a man sent for a girl it meant interest, interest which could hardly mean less than marriage . . .

The lieutenant said, graciously, 'I bought a paper before leaving. A Gin County sheet.' It was in his hand, a single sheet no more than ten inches deep. 'There's not much in it — it gets smaller. But you can have it if you want.'

McGaughey said, 'Thanks.' He wanted to dream on about the girl, wanted to relive those delicious moments holding her the previous night. But he must be diplomatic in face of the officer's friendliness. 'But I don't feel like reading.'

'Neither do I.' The lieutenant hadn't wanted him to read, anyway, and his tone was hearty. He looked at the sheet, as if dismissing it. 'The war news is so bad you don't want to read about it. We're getting the hell of a licking all over the place, but it won't last — we'll chase the Rebs right into the Gulf before we're through.'

He was quite a nice young officer, but he couldn't quite forget he was an officer. There was a slight note of condescension about his friendliness and McGaughey didn't miss it. He wasn't offended; slightly amused, rather.

'There's more news about the Buie incident — the only other interesting item of news.' Talking about it was one way of easing into conversation with the trooper. Questioning could come later, McGaughey thought ironically.

'The Buie incident?' He tried to be helpful.

But having said it was interesting as a news item, now the lieutenant spoke rather deprecatingly about it.

'Oh, it's just another of those lynchings. A man up Shondon Valley — that's eight or nine miles up river from Gin Point — got his neck stretched for presumed Southern sympathies.' The lieutenant let the newspaper flutter away. 'They did a thorough job of it, by all accounts — burned him out afterwards, his whole darned farm.'

McGaughey said, 'We had some lynchings like that over in Erlington County. But not recently. Just when the war began extremists started to tar and feather, lynch and libel. But they didn't get things all their own way and after a time they stopped bothering about trifles.'

'You think they're trifles?'

'The necks of a few supposed Reb sympathisers? With thousands dying in battles down the Mississippi valley and in Virginia and other places?'

McGaughey put his answer in the form of a question, and the lieutenant didn't quite like it. This trooper was too sure of himself, too certain in his opinions. Lieutenant Alabastor found himself rather preferring men who waited to hear his opinion before making their own known — and then diffidently modifying theirs to make it not too disagreeable to the lieutenant.

Abruptly he asked, 'You lived in Erlington County?'

McGaughey thought, 'This is where the questions begin!' and steeled himself to give little away in his replies.

He nodded. Alabastor's thin brown intelligent face frowned. 'Why didn't you join a local regiment?'

'Most people don't bother to ask that; they say outright, 'Why are you, a surgeon, content to ride as an ordinary cavalry trooper?'' McGaughey said drily. He was mildly enjoying himself, playing with this boy officer. Yet Alabastor, in years, could hardly have been younger than he.

'Well, why did you, then?' The lieutenant was even less sure about this conversation, liked even less the way McGaughey seemed to direct the talk.

And he found himself resenting this lazy, tolerant attitude of the trooper's which suggested that he, the officer, was of inferior mental calibre.

McGaughey shrugged. 'You've got to have friends before you get a surgeon's job in the army. You've got to have important people support your claims for a commission. And if you can't get that support — ' He shrugged again.

Alabastor stared. 'But weren't you in practice? Couldn't you call upon local judges, parsons, attorneys?' He couldn't understand all this. It seemed elementary to him.

'I couldn't.' McGaughey's tone became short. 'And I'm sorry, I can't tell you why.' The lieutenant saw thinning lips, eyes that smiled but weren't friendly. He began to wish he hadn't started this conversation.

Then McGaughey took pity on him. He wasn't bad as a man or as an officer. When the time came the lieutenant had behaved decisively, courageously, he remembered. He said, 'It won't hurt me to ride trooper for a year or so. It's quite something to live for the day and not have commitments for any longer.'

'But you're a Harvard man.' Alabaster was friendly again, insistent though. 'You're wasted here. It's the finest university in the land.'

'The finest medical school, anyway,' McGaughey accepted. He smiled suddenly. 'But they don't know everything at Harvard, lootenant. On some matters they're as blind and ignorant as the army.'

The lieutenant was smiling slightly, doubtfully, not sure that this wasn't faintly seditious talk. His eyes were questioning.

McGaughey hitched up his pants. 'Flat feet,' he smiled. 'Darn it, the army and Harvard both say flat-footed men are no good for the army. So they don't get in.'

'Well, are they?'

'We're blind, lootenant.' The trooper's voice was impressively earnest. 'All round us we can see that both are wrong. Every barefooted wharf labourer has flat feet, every darned one of 'em. But does it affect them? No, sir! They can walk all day and run like the devil when they have to!'

Alabastor shook his head, faintly bewildered. He spoke the truth, 'I'm afraid I don't understand anything about medical matters.'

He was rising. McGaughey looked up at him and took a risk. His soft voice asked, 'Does our regimental surgeon?'

The lieutenant halted. He could have taken exception to that question about a brother officer from a trooper, but he didn't. He merely said, 'That's not a question I wish to answer, trooper.' Then he went off to arrange about a sentry for the nights watches.

McGaughey took advantage of the last of the sunshine, smiled and stretched on his back and looked into a cloudless sky that was deepening to purple with the approach of night. The lieutenant didn't think much of their regimental surgeon either, evidently.

Who could? He was probably a quack without any real medical training, a man who had got his commission through influence. There were many like him. It would be a good day when only qualified men were able to call themselves doctor, he was thinking.

His thoughts went back to the girl. He wished he knew her name. If he had known it he would have lain there repeating it over and over again. With a start he realised that it was a long time since he had found himself thinking of a girl as much as this one. And he hardly knew her.

He got up and found it was becoming chilly. He must watch himself; he was getting romantic ideas, he thought. He'd seen many a good man go like that, and before they knew where they were they were saddled with a wife and a family too big for them to support.

He saw a fluttering sheet of paper and went across to retrieve it. A piece of paper could do an almighty lot of damage where skittery mules and horses were concerned. He didn't want to search half the county for a bolting horse.

He thought, 'I must watch out. There must be no sending back for the girl!' She'd think one thing if he did — that he was all-fired interested in her, and that would never do.

McGaughey sighed. Why, he thought, couldn't a man love a girl without marriage posing itself as a problem?

The two sly-looking troopers came crashing through the undergrowth down the hill. They looked furtively around for the officer, and when they saw he wasn't about they went quickly across to the fire and carefully placed something in the embers.

Eggs, thought McGaughey. They were roasting eggs that had belonged to a Dutch farmer a few minutes before. Well, the farmer was lucky he hadn't lost his daughter, too.

He went across and reached into the fire for an egg. The two troopers looked evilly at him but said nothing as he began to shell the egg. They couldn't for fear of drawing the officer's attention upon themselves. McGaughey said, 'Nice eggs you thieved. Let me know next time you get some, will you?'

It tickled his sense of humour to see the scowls and black looks. It made the egg taste better, standing there idly looking at that newspaper. There was little enough in it, as the lieutenant had said. More reverses at Richmond. Thousands of men lost in the retreat from the Rebels' capital that had so nearly fallen in the first Union advance.

'McClellan's not up to it,' he thought. The Confederate generals, Robert E. Lee and Stonewall Jackson, were far more brilliant.

His eye caught the words, 'The Buie Lynching.' But he wasn't interested. These cases were only interesting if you knew the people concerned, he thought. He was only mildly surprised when he read that Marshal Thomas Henderson, peace officer for Gin

County, was still actively investigating the affair.

What was there to investigate in a straightforward lynching? McGaughey thought. Then he had a picture of a heavy man wearing a wide-brimmed old straw hat. He wondered if that was Marshal Tom Henderson. He remembered his impression of intelligence; that marshal didn't look the kind of man to waste his time.

The picket on top of the hill shouted down at that moment. They couldn't see him because of the trees, but the lieutenant came crawling out of his tent immediately. He saw the troopers around the fire, preparing their bed rolls — there were no tents for troopers on this journey — and he called, 'What was that about?'

No one was very disturbed. This was not territory hostile to Union forces. McGaughey shouted, 'I'll go up and see — sir.' He went clambering up the hillside under the trees. It was very dark here, screened from the reflecting rays of a sun just set. All at once the trooper came out on top of the hill.

The sentry was standing there, looking northwards. He was fully exposed and because he was leaning on his gun McGaughey realised that whatever the cause of that cry it represented no immediate danger to the camp.

McGaughey walked across to him. The man turned, recognised him and straightway pointed across the immense night-misted basin towards the rolling hills on the Minnesota border.

'Look!' McGaughey saw several pin points of red in the distance. 'Fires!'

The sentry spat lugubriously. 'Big fires, I reckon. Now what started them?' It was too early for prairie fires, for the land was still green from the spring rains.

McGaughey started to report back to his officer, but Alabastor and the rugged, silent sergeant were just toiling up the steep hillside. McGaughey called down to them, 'There's three or four fires about twenty miles distant. Must be big for them to be seen from here.'

'Are they together?' McGaughey could see the white oval that was the lieutenant's face in the gloom under the trees. The light was going rapidly.

'No. Must be miles apart, I'd say.'

The whole camp toiled up to have a look at the mysterious fires, all except the two furtive-eyed men who took this opportunity to roast their loot and scoff it quickly before anyone else could demand a share. There was speculation, then everyone remembered their tiredness from a day in the saddle and all went quickly down to their blankets.

In the night — not much before dawn — a sentry heard someone galloping hard up to the Dutch farm. He reported this when he was questioned by Lieutenant Alabastor next morning. The rider hadn't tarried there, but had gone galloping on after a few minutes.

That questioning was after the lieutenant had discovered that the Dutch farm had been deserted in the night.

7

Jackie Bullen, Alabastor's orderly, came running into the camp even before the sun was up. He was a fresh-faced boy, willing and friendly, in awe of his officer and at all times going out of his way to please him.

He had been called before dawn to get the lieutenant's breakfast and shaving water ready and had gone across to the farm with a can for some milk for the officer's coffee and perhaps some eggs.

He was perplexed as he ran in. He didn't like to speak about the matter to the lieutenant in case he was making a fool of himself, but he told some of the men, sitting up shivering in their dew-drenched blankets.

'There's no one at the farm. No one at all. Everyone's up an' gone.'

The men weren't interested. They

were concerned about getting into their boots and finding a drink for their dry, unpleasant-tasting mouths. They growled, what of it? Maybe the folk had gone out to tend the animals.

The boy shook his head. He came from farming stock himself. The cows were standing at the gate, he told them, bawling mournfully to be milked. Farmers didn't go off leaving cows unmilked like that. Besides, the door was open and the place was in disorder.

McGaughey heard and came across at that. He was looking at the two unprepossessing men who had been sneaking around that farm the previous evening. They were hard cases and he wouldn't put anything past them. What if they had gone up in the night — after the farmer's daughter maybe — had been discovered and committed a graver crime than egg stealing?

The two men were pulling on their boots, sitting on disordered blankets. It seemed to McGaughey that they avoided his gaze when he looked across at them.

He told the orderly, 'Waken the lootenant. Report this matter to him.' And his voice was a command; he had a habit of giving orders, some of the men had already found out.

Alabastor rose promptly and went to investigate. The farm was deserted and in confusion. It was quite a mystery. He took to questioning the sentries. The last one on before dawn told of the mysterious night rider.

'And then what happened?'

'A light came on. It stayed on till daylight.' Alabastor nodded. That lamp had still been lit when he entered the farmhouse. 'Its sounded like a cart moved off a half-hour later.'

That was all the sentry knew. Alabastor said, 'It seems they decided to quit in the night. Just up and left the place.' He was perplexed. People didn't quit just like that, not in his experience. He looked round at his men suspiciously, wondering if they had anything to do with it. In that early light, rough, unwashed and unshaven, they merited suspicion.

But there was nothing he could do about the matter. If a man chose to leave his farm wide open, it was none of his business.

They breakfasted, loaded up the lead horses, mounted and took the trail again. After half an hour they were clear of trees momentarily and had a broad view of the basin beyond. Involuntarily all stopped, gazing onto the valley bottom. A trail ran the length of that valley, a trail as yet bordered by only a few new farms. They could see crude dwellings in cleared spaces among the clumps of trees.

But what attracted their attention was the movement on that distant trail.

The whole length of it was dotted with crawling vehicles all heading south. They could see coloured patches which were cattle being driven amongst the wagons, and specks which their trained eyes told them were people on foot.

Alabastor swore under his breath. 'Now, what does that mean?' he asked the silent, battered-faced sergeant sitting alongside him. The sergeant didn't know. The time was long past when they might expect to see an immigrant train of this size on the move in these parts. Besides, the lieutenant quickly thought, this straggly column was moving the wrong way. The new lands open to settlers were north and west, in Minnesota and Dakota, Kansas, Nebraska and distant Colorado.

He scratched his head. This morning was full of perplexities. He gave the order to strike straight across towards that trail, though he had been intending a different route, heading rather more northwards towards the Atchison Agency.

An hour or so later they came up on to the trail and rested their blown horses while a weary train of assorted wagons came lumbering slowly towards them. The men, including their young officer, were all leaning forward, watching intently, even a little excitedly.

The first wagon was an old canvas-topped prairie schooner that looked as if it had been lying neglected behind a farmhouse for months. Tied all about it were chests and cases, chairs and even a table. The men had never seen a prairie wagon so loaded.

'Looks like someone's movin',' a voice said among the waiting cavalrymen.

'Looks like a hull durned country's movin',' someone else retorted.

All those wagons — high, two-wheeled farm carts, mule carts, buggies, anything that moved on wheels — were loaded to overflowing like the first. In among them farm stock were being driven, and weary people trudged on foot.

They saw a silent people approaching, walking or slumping on the wagons. There was an air of hopelessness, of defeat about them that wasn't understandable. At the sight of their blue uniforms, however, some life seemed to come back to some of them, and a few horsemen came cantering ahead of the noisy, grinding vehicles.

The lieutenant saluted. These men were rough-clothed, bearded like farmers. Alabastor jerked his head in astonishment towards the procession. 'What's all this about?'

'You ain't heerd?' Sardonic eyes gazed at the officer. He shook his head. Then they told him.

The Sioux were rampaging out of the reservations. The previous day they had stormed along the Flagstaff Ridge, killing all white folk in their path, and burning their newly-built farmhouses.

That explained a lot. The fires the previous evening and, Alabastor now thought, that mysterious rider in the night followed by the Dutch family's hasty flight . . . that had been a warning, and the Dutch people had been quick to act upon it.

Alabastor swore angrily to himself.

Why the devil hadn't the man the grace to come and pass on the warning to the detail? There wasn't such a panic of a hurry that it couldn't have been done.

He led his men off the trail, quickened their pace and struck out northwards. All the way they passed fleeing settlers with their families and their few prized possessions. It was a saddening, sickening sight. These people had thought the Indian wars were over, that their new lands, won from Nature by such hard toil and sacrifice, were safe from invasion. They looked stunned, some of them, as if they couldn't believe that after all they had been forced to abandon their holdings and were lucky to be here with their lives.

'As if a civil war isn't enough without an Indian uprising,' Alabastor was thinking, and sight of those refugees seemed to make him angry. His tone was very bitter when he spoke to his men.

He questioned many of the refugees

as they came up with them, wanting to know the situation so that he could send a report back to his HQ at Gin Point.

For a long time the story hardly varied. Gallant citizens had come riding to warn the outlying farms, calling that the Indians were on the rampage and if they wished to save their lives they had better flee while they could. That had been the previous evening. The settlers had seen distant farmhouses going up in flames, getting nearer, so they had acted on the advice, packed hurriedly, and were now heading for the safety of the garrison towns along the Gin River.

Towards noon, when the fleeing column was thinning, they saw the first of the wounded. A buggy was driving pretty fast from the hills. In it were three men. They were holding their guns and looking very grim. McGaughey was quick to notice the bandaged arms, the bloody shirts, the crude rag of a bandage on one of the heads.

Alabastor halted the buggy, and the men were glad to rest their jaded nag for a few moments. The blue uniforms were reassuring, even though the detail was small in number.

'You've been in action against the Sioux?' The men nodded. McGaughey passed across his canteen and the men drank gratefully. 'How many are in the outbreak? I want all the information you can give me.' These men might be able to supply positive information; if so he would be able to get his report back to the regiment.

The weary, wounded men began to tell their story. McGaughey got into their buggy while they spoke and examined their wounds. None had been hurt badly, but at least he was able to make them more comfortable.

So far as they knew, the whole Sioux nation had come pouring out of their several reserves. They hadn't received the spring ration of food or the bounty promised by the Government and they were fighting mad, the wounded men told them. They had taken part in some rearguard actions with other settlers to give these wagons chance to escape out of the country. Now the Indians seemed to have gone north a bit, towards Flagstaff City. They, rendered useless by their wounds, were heading south out of the troubled area.

'All out!' The troopers murmured and whistled under their breath at the news, and now their faces were anxious as they looked suspiciously into the northern hills.

That could mean that anything up to five thousand Sioux warriors were right now on the war trail, maybe no more than a few miles from them. There was an immediate checking of guns and ammunition, a tightening of belts and in general an instinctive preparation for a fight.

But the men weren't wanting a clash with five thousand Sioux and they said so, and they took care to let their voices lift high enough for the lieutenant to hear. A few of them at this moment discovered that they had joined up to fight Confederates, and opined it was no part of their contract to be pitchforked into battle with scalp-hunting Sioux.

The lieutenant took no notice of them. He was busy writing a report back to HQ. That done, a man was detailed to ride hell-for-leather back to Gin Point with the despatch. As the newest and therefore the least-trained recruit, McGaughey might have expected to be made messenger, but Alabastor passed him over. 'There's going to be need for your surgical skill, McGaughey,' he said, and that was the nearest to humour they had ever heard from the lieutenant.

That same trooper took a note, terse and commanding, from McGaughey to Sergeant Gehler.

Then he gave the order to ride on. There was some uneasy growling from the men. Two sly-eyed, egg-filled troopers were especially concerned about their skins and were disposed to argue. Twenty men riding into territory overrun by thousands of heathen, murdering Sioux? They were aghast.

But it didn't occur to the lieutenant to retire. His orders had been to take this detail to the Atchison Agency. He was compromising a little now by heading for Flagstaff City, but there was no thought of retreat in his mind. When he heard the growls of alarm and discontent, Alabastor spoke sharply to his sergeant.

Then the discontented found another man who wasn't prepared to argue against orders. That battered-faced, normally-silent sergeant erupted into a torrent of sound. He called the men names they hadn't heard in a long while, and the threats he made if he heard any more grousing were lurid and impressive. The detail rode on without murmur after that.

By mid-afternoon they were in rolling country, with plenty of greenery to offer cover to ambushers. It made for nervy riding, every man on the watch, every finger wrapped round the trigger of their rifles. Long ago they had passed the last of the refugees — all wounded — and they didn't expect to see any more.

The next human being they saw, everyone felt, would be a war-painted war-bonneted Sioux warrior!

Yet time went by and there was nothing to disturb them. Gradually it dawned on them that that wounded man in the buggy had been right when he opined that the Sioux war trail had turned northwards towards Flagstaff. Well, they would soon know for certain. They should reach Flagstaff by evening.

When they were a few miles from Flagstaff, just dropping down from the hills on to the Flagstaff plain, they began to hear sounds of distant firing. They halted. Ahead of them was good farmland, all under cultivation, with livestock out in the fields. In the distance, on the Flagstaff River, they could see the town. It was quite a size, and some of the men said there were three or four thousand people living there. McGaughey thought more would be there now, with refugees in from all the surrounding district.

They moved on to the open plain cautiously, alert for first signs of the enemy. As they passed the farmsteads they saw that all were deserted. There were unmistakeable signs, too, that the Indians had been this way, for a lot of the animals were dead or injured, wantonly assailed by the Indians who hadn't bothered to stop and use the animals for food.

They saw no other dead, and guessed that the settlers had been wise and had retreated at the first alarm into Flagstaff City instead of trying to stand off the Sioux on their isolated farms.

When they were within a mile of Flagstaff Alabastor quickened his pace. He saw now that the fighting was to the west and north of the town, and it seemed an opportunity for the detail to slip into Flagstaff unobserved. They could see sentries at the end of barricaded streets waving to them, and the action seemed reassuring.

They went into the town at a rush. As they came up, hundreds of citizens, mostly women and children, Alabastor noticed, gathered to cheer them in. Perhaps the citizens thought this was the advance guard of a bigger relief column.

The barricades were dragged to one side to let them ride into the town, then were replaced hurriedly behind them. With cheering people running at their stirrups, the lieutenant walked their horses in towards the centre of the town, until they came to an open square where stood a spired church, an obvious school house, offices and some shops pretty well up to the standard of Gin Point.

The square was crowded, though few of the people there had much time for spectating. There was a busy hurrying to and fro upon some mission in connection with the defence of the town. Men were running in little groups, bringing up fresh ammunition or taking food out to the defenders or going up as reinforcements. Wounded were trickling in to be received by a hospital group who got them away for treatment.

The atmosphere was tense, the soldiers felt. For all their defence preparations, the place was uneasy, fearful. As they scurried about their business, people watched quickly over their shoulders, as if expecting to see wild Sioux warriors at any moment pouring into the town.

Yet the mayor's statement, when he came to greet them, was reassuring. He came threading his way through the crowd as the troopers dismounted stiffly and pumped water into a wooden trough for their jaded, thirsty beasts. He was hatless, a greying, elderly man, short and heavy and with an air of calmness about him that was good to see.

There was a light of pleasure in his eyes as he held out his hand to the lieutenant. 'Glad to see you, lootenant. I hope there's more cavalry right behind you.'

Alabastor shook his head. 'Not unless a report of mine brings some up from Gin Point.'

'Too bad. Still, I reckon the town will be glad to see you, all the same.' The smile was genuinely glad.

'What's the situation? I heard firing all the way in?'

The mayor shrugged. 'The Sioux are out there.' He nodded northwards. 'There are thousands of them, and they're all armed. They've tasted blood and they won't be held back.'

'But they're not yet attacking the town in earnest?'

'Nope. That's the Injun way, I reckon. They're after loot, for the moment. But when they're satisfied with that — ' He shrugged.

He told them that so far they had had only skirmishes with the Sioux. 'We called in the people from all across the plains when we heard the

Sioux were out. The Sioux have been foraying on all sides of the town, burning and destroying, but only occasionally making any direct attack upon us.

'Hear that?' There was a brief pause of gunfire over the northern buildings. 'Them Sioux sneak in as close as they can get, then start to fire on the town. We've lost a few men that way — a lot more wounded — but not more than you would expect.'

'And if they attack the town?'

Again the mayor shrugged. 'We're a big place to defend, an' I reckon some of our people have lost their spunk. I guess the Sioux could overrun us if they attacked determinedly enough.' His eyes twinkled. 'Better get them reinforcements up pretty quick, lootenant, or you might wish you hadn't come to Flagstaff.'

The lieutenant gave some orders to the cavalry sergeant and then walked away with the mayor to inspect the defences. A man came up and said the soldiers could bed out in the school. They were using it as a hospital, but there was plenty of room for them at the moment.

Leaving their horses in a livery stable, the troopers took up their bedrolls and crossed the square. Smoke was drifting thickly into the town now. The Sioux must have fired a sizeable building to windward of Flagstaff City.

They found the school. Some women attending upon the wounded received them gladly. They were afraid, but they weren't showing it, and McGaughey saw they were doing a pretty good job of nursing, for amateurs. He found that a big basement under the school, cool within its whitewashed walls, had been turned into a hospital ward. Beds had been taken down, and a dozen of them were already occupied with wounded. Professional curiosity took him along to see them. A man came into the cellar after him.

He was small, spare, elderly and not too quick in his movements. He looked at McGaughey and said, 'What do you want down here, soldier?' But his voice wasn't unfriendly, only tired.

McGaughey told him, 'Like yourself, I'm a doctor.' He lifted his hands as the doctor registered surprise. 'Sure, I'm only a trooper, but that's the truth of it, as you can soon find out. Now, if there's anything I can do to help . . . ' He smiled upon the tired man.

'My name's Lockland, Stephen Lockland.' The doctor held out his hand. If there were any doubts in his mind, he was too polite to show them. 'Perhaps you'll be more needed as a soldier and not as a doctor,' he smiled.

'Tomorrow, perhaps. But tonight I don't think so.'

McGaughey was looking at a patient, a middle-aged man with pallid features and the dead eyes of a man nearly out of the world with pain. Dr. Lockland drew back a blanket. A bloody bandage was wrapped around the man's knee.

'Bad?' asked McGaughey softly.

'It will have to come off,' Lockland

said. His eyes became thoughtful. 'He was brought in an hour ago. His knee was smashed by a bullet. I intended to operate this evening. Have you done much surgical work?'

'Enough,' McGaughey was brief. 'I'll get my lootenant's permission to help you. I guess you'll be needing assistance.'

Then McGaughey realised that Lockland was first waiting for information about himself. 'How did you get your training?'

'At Harvard.' Lockland's eyes lit up at that. A Harvard man. There was no better in America at that time. But McGaughey saw an unvoiced question in the elderly doctor's eyes, guessed what it was and answered it for him. 'My name's McGaughey, James Clarke McGaughey.'

Doctor Lockland's hand went down to his side. Without hesitation he said, 'Erlington County?'

'The same.' Here was a man who had heard of him, knew of his past. But the doctor said nothing more on the subject. As if his curiosity was at an end he turned away, saying, 'We'll fix up an operating table over there.'

He indicated a door in the white-washed wall which probably gave into an adjoining, smaller room.

'It has a good light. Plenty of windows.' The doctor said, 'I'm short of drugs, short of bandage. Short of everything. Worst of all, I've less than a pint of ether.' As if the thought had just struck him — 'Do you use ether?'

'I prefer chloroform. Ether upsets the patient too much. But I know some doctors prefer it,' McGaughey added diplomatically. He said, 'I'll find the lootenant. The army doesn't take kindly to men taking on jobs without authority.'

He started to walk away. He knew as he walked out of that ward that the doctor was watching him all the way. He wondered what expression would be on that old face. Doubt? Suspicion? Condemnation . . . ?

McGaughey shrugged. 'The hell with what people think,' he told himself. It was only when they came with guns that a man needed to worry. He was very tired, saddle-stiff and hungry, but he began to whistle. There was need for him here, and he was looking forward to resuming his old profession of doctor.

One of the troopers, a man of Swedish ancestry inevitably named Olson, growled from where he was sitting on his blankets, 'You sound cheerful, soldier.' His head jerked towards a fresh burst of gunfire outside. 'That ain't a noise to cheer any man, I reckon. So why are you whistlin'?' His voice was almost a complaint.

'Because I feel good.'

'An' why do you feel good?'

'Because,' Trooper McGaughey said, stiff-faced, 'I'm just going to cut a man's leg off.'

He went in search of the lieutenant. Olson looked after him shook his head. 'Dat ain't no yoke,' he said, and again his voice was filled with grievance.

McGaughey found the lieutenant with the town's defence committee, crouching against a barricade of heavy logs across one end of a street leading northwards out of the town. There was only a little firing now, as if with the decline of the sun the Sioux were tiring of skirmishing.

The lieutenant was saying, 'Today's been a holiday for the Sioux. They've been gorging their starving bellies, drinking where they can find liquor, and hunting for stray ammunition. Tomorrow they will have sore heads: they'll call in their scattered forces and attempt to storm the town. You see if I'm not right.'

The committee was in agreement with the cavalry officer. Someone proposed that they try to get women and children out of Flagstaff County in the night, but there was no enthusiasm for the idea. It meant splitting forces, and if the refugees blundered on to a Sioux camp in the dark . . .

McGaughey caught the lieutenant's eye. 'What is it, McGaughey?'

'There's only one doctor to look after the wounded. He looks tuckered in and I'd like to help him with some operations.'

The lieutenant said immediately, 'Do what you can.' Then he added, 'I'll come and watch you work. What are you going to do? Amputate?' McGaughey nodded. 'That should be interesting. I've never witnessed an amputation before.'

McGaughey performed that operation. He started by acting as anesthetist, holding an ether-soaked sponge over the face of the patient. But when he saw the older doctor's trembling hand he said, sharply, 'You're in no condition for operating. You're tired out, man. Let me do it.'

Doctor Lockland was not averse. He had been without sleep for two whole days now, for on the night before the Indian scare he had been attending a dying patient across the river. He handed over his surgeon's knife and took McGaughey's place with the ether sponge.

McGaughey began to amputate. The patient was groaning heavily under that anesthetic. The sickly fumes filled the little whitewashed storeroom. The lieutenant watched, fascinated, the blood draining from his face, mouth moving with the horror of that sight.

Then he went quickly out, brought back the meal he had eaten hastily before the operation, and felt in no need for further food that night. Never again was he condescending towards McGaughey after that.

* * *

Daylight showed the western bank of the Flagstaff River to be alive with Indians. There were thousands of them, running and riding in from all directions.

'They're massing for an attack on the town,' Lieutenant Alabastor told his men. 'There's a movement north of the river to strike across and surround Flagstaff. When that happens it will become a fight for our lives; we'll have to hold out until reinforcements are sent up to us.'

It wasn't a cheering situation. Flagstaff might have several thousand population, but two-thirds of these would be women, children and girls, many sick, aged and infirm — and many without heart for battle against the savage, murdering Indians.

And on that plain even the most optimistic could not see less than five thousand fighting Sioux, superb warriors who had twice within the past few years fought United States armies and defeated them in pitched battle.

McGaughey had to go to the barricades with the other troopers. But Lockland had been able to sleep that night and was for the moment, at any rate, well able to cope with the wounded.

There were troopers marching through the town when they heard shouts across the square. They saw horsemen cantering in from a street that led eastwards across the Flagstaff Plain. It was that same street down which they had walked their horses the previous day.

The troopers watched them in the distance. McGaughey heard one man growl, 'Looks like a party's ridden in for safety. They got in just in time.'

Another trooper spat at that. 'In time for what? Massacre?'

They were a poor lot of soldiers, McGaughey thought critically. Too many grousers had been picked for this detail . . .

Hours passed. The Sioux were still massing and deploying out there on the sunlit plain. By now everyone reckoned they would have completely encircled the town. But still there was no fighting.

In mid-morning Alabastor sent half the men back for rest and a meal. There seemed no sense in having the entire defence at the barricades under that blazing summer's sun, and he was a thoughtful officer.

McGaughey tramped back with the party. A field kitchen had been set up at the south end of the square, and there was plenty of hot food and drink for the taking. There was no fear of this garrison being starved out, McGaughey thought, accepting a huge hunk of bread and a steaming bowl of meaty soup.

He carried it away carefully, searching for a seat. He saw the low wall around the schoolhouse and gingerly made his way across. There was quite a picnic atmosphere here, with lots of men and women taking their food — settlers in from the outlying farms who had nowhere else to sit in this town . . .

McGaughey saw someone standing in the doorway of the schoolhouse looking towards him. The soup slopped over the bowl rim, burning his fingers. Involuntarily he exclaimed, 'What in heaven's name! How did you get here?'

The girl was running across towards him, her face smiling, alight with pleasure.

8

He set the bowl down on the wall and wiped his hand. But when she came near she seemed shy to shake it. She was crimsoning, now that she was close to him, her eyes fluttering uncertainly, never daring to remain on his face. She was the picture of embarrassment and it was McGaughey who was the first to speak.

'Now, how did you get yourself into Flagstaff?' His voice echoed with astonishment. He could still hardly believe his eyes.

'I rode in a few hours ago. I found a party of settlers who had been in the Gin Valley and were anxious to get to their families, here in Flagstaff.'

Her voice, troubled and uncertain, was like music to his ears. He took her hand and made her sit on the wall. He knew his eyes were shining, showing nakedly his delight at seeing her, however unexpected.

'I — I enquired, found you were billeted in the schoolhouse, so — ' Her voice trailed away. So she had stood there the past few hours waiting for his return.

For seconds he could only stare at her, his mind a conflict of emotions. He still didn't understand how she had found him, what she was doing here so soon after he had left her. But more than that, he was trying to adjust his thoughts towards her.

He couldn't help feeling pleased to see her, and yet there was a disturbance in his mind. It wasn't usual for girls to come following a man. It could mean a depth of feeling that was flattering but yet would be embarrassing. He felt uneasy as to the outcome of this situation . . .

They heard just then a swelling roar on the outskirts of the town. Everyone stopped eating and looked up, frowning, anxious. Some people began to go towards the sound, as if to seek its cause.

'Sounds like our folk at the barricades are mighty angry about something,' a red-faced settler said, tearing into a hunk of cold meat and then hurriedly swilling down the food with hot, strong-smelling coffee. He listened anxiously, but made no move to leave the square.

McGaughey said, 'Looks like things are opening up. I'd better get on with this — ' He indicated his soup and bread. 'Meanwhile, tell me what happened when you found I had gone out on detail from Gin Barracks.'

He began to eat hurriedly, listening to that roar of anger that grew louder with every passing second. It seemed to be spreading, encircling the town completely within minutes.

The girl told him — 'I didn't know you'd gone out, but a sergeant came looking for me among the laundresses.'

'He had a bad eye?'

'Well, he was holding a handkerchief to it most of the time.' Gehler. 'He told me you had left for the Atchison Agency. He gave me your message.'

'Message?' McGaughey was floundering out of his depth. He had left no message with Gehler; that note he had sent probably hadn't yet reached the man!

'And — and your five dollars.' Her eyes were downcast, otherwise she might have noticed the blank astonishment on that lean, brown face. She looked up. 'It was nice of you to think of me, to send me that money. But you needn't have done. I have a little money by me.'

McGaughey took a deep breath. 'Take it gently,' he advised. 'Tell me what that double-crossing Gehler did — tell me everything from the beginning.'

But there wasn't much more for him to know, only to have the points emphasised and put in order.

Gehler must have gone looking for the girl even while the detail was parading. He had seemed nervous, she remembered, had been very urgent in his tone.

Trooper McGaughey had sent him. McGaughey was going for duty up to the reserves. He wanted her to follow as quickly as she could and here were five dollars to help her on her way. McGaughey choked.

Gehler had got rid of two embarrassments, he thought, and suddenly his anger left him: the situation tickled his sense of humour. Poor Gehler, scared of what outrageous demands might come from a trooper, had shown unexpected powers of resource and cunning!

'I went back home. I thought it would be safe enough. I packed a bundle of things and left a note in case Frank returned.' But it had been a hopeless gesture McGaughey guessed; she must surely now believe that her brother had fallen to foul play or she would have heard from him by now.

She had found a freight cart travelling to Bembrock, and had got another lift on a wagon out of the Gin Valley. Then they had got news of the Sioux uprising. The wagoner had halted then, refusing to go on. When the first of the refugee wagons came pouring down the trail the wagoner had turned about and gone with them.

'But you didn't go?'

'I felt I wanted to get through to you.' She met his eyes. 'Don't think badly of me, please, but things have happened lately . . . twice.' Her voce broke. 'I feel weak and terrified and in danger.'

His hand clasped over hers. 'You were in danger.'

'But I don't feel in danger with you.' She had to tell him that, but now again she averted her eyes. 'That's how I felt above Bembrock. All I could think was that things would be all right, I wouldn't be frightened any more, if I found you again. And you had sent for me,' she said simply. 'If you thought it was safer for me to be with you, then I was determined to find you.'

McGaughey went quickly back to his

soup. He had a guilty feeling; he hadn't sent for the girl, and he could imagine her embarrassment if she knew the truth. He urged her to tell the rest of her story.

While she was standing by the side of that dusty trail, with its procession of forlorn refugees plodding southwards, some settlers came riding up from the Gin Valley. They'd heard of the Sioux peril and were concerned for their families over on the Flagstaff Plain. She had begged a lift and they took her in turns behind them.

'When we reached the town I heard that a detail of cavalry had ridden in yesterday. I guessed it was yours.' She was smiling, feeling pleased with herself now her story was ended. He finished his meal. She was watching him anxiously, as if feeling a constraint in his manner.

So, suddenly, he lifted his head and smiled at her. 'I'm glad to see you again . . . '

His face stopped smiling. There was a

crackle of rifle fire from several points around the town. He saw his comrades grab their guns and begin to race back across the square. Men were shouting, running from the houses to take up battle stations. Women were getting panicky, searching for playing children. There was noise and confusion everywhere.

'I've got to go,' McGaughey shouted above the din. 'Stay by the schoolhouse so that I can find you.'

He picked up his rifle and was about to race away to the barricades, when he remembered something. His smiling face turned back towards her.

'Darn it, always I forget to ask you. What's your name?'

'Sara Buie.' She was smiling back at him. His pulse was racing. He was glad she had found her way to Flagstaff, could even forgive the cunning ungrateful Sergeant Gehler for what he had done.

Sara. He found himself repeating the name as he ran through the alleys to where he had left the lieutenant. A nice name, nicer than Sarah. Buie. Another nice name.

Buie? He said the name again to himself, frowning as he ran to where white powder smoke came drifting back from the defenders firing rapidly at the barricades. He had heard that name before.

The lieutenant saw the returning party and shouted, 'On to the roofs!'

McGaughey took a jump and dragged himself on to a low wall. He heaved and pulled himself on to a sloping roof of a single-storeyed cottage. And then he remembered.

The Buie lynching. He had seen the name only a couple of days before in the Gin County news-sheet . . .

A form suddenly reared before him, twisted then fell across his back. When McGaughey shoved him away he saw it was a settler, dead already from a bullet wound in the head. He moved with caution after that.

A short, thick plank rested in the

gutter, its other end providing a firing point over the ridge of the shingled roof. McGaughey clambered cautiously into the position so recently occupied by that dead settler, and peered beyond.

His first impression was of a lot of smoke on the flat land beyond. He realised that homesteads all over the plain had been fired by the Indians. Now he could understand that swelling roar of anger that had risen from the townspeople at the barricades. It had been caused by this orgy of destruction. The Indians, thought McGaughey, must have done it deliberately to infuriate their enemies. Then he realised there might be another intention.

The thick smoke was blowing almost on to the town where the river wound away at the north end. He guessed that the Sioux were taking advantage of the smoke cloud to crawl close up to the city defences.

There was some fighting along to his right, but no great activity immediately before him. The marksman who had got that unfortunate settler must have been shot in turn or gone away.

McGaughey grew bolder and took risks in order to see the scene beyond the town. He felt an eager excitement inside him; he had wondered if he would feel afraid when the battle started but now found he didn't. There was just an intense curiosity, a desire to watch and see everything at once.

He saw the hedged fields on that gently undulating plain, pleasant in their variegated greens and with the occasional yellow patches of early ripening corn. About a mile away, where a few trees stood on some high ground, a large force of Indians was congregated. There were many ponies grazing at the foot of the hill, and McGaughey thought this would be the Indian cavalry, held in reserve to exploit any breakthrough made into the town's defences by the Sioux infantry.

He was disturbed to see small knots of men walking and riding towards that knoll from several directions. Reinforcements for the Sioux were still coming up.

His gaze shifted closer. He looked over cottage gardens, green with vegetables and bright with flowers. Saw isolated cottages straggling away towards those fields, and shook his head. It would have been better if those cottages had been fired by the townspeople yesterday. But he could imagine the objections of the owners.

Still, now those sheds and cottages could act as stepping stones for the Indian infantry when they set up an attack on this side of the town.

He realised that the farthermost building, a stone-built farmhouse, was stoutly barricaded and defended. Occasionally he saw puffs of smoke from shuttered windows. No doubt that defence post was designed to keep the Indians from using those other buildings as cover for an advance on the town, but McGaughey shook his head.

They were brave men to stay out

there, but he felt sure in time the Indians would crawl past the defence post and either wipe out the occupants or simply ignore it and carry the fight closer to the main barricades.

Lying there with the hot sun pouring uncomfortably upon his back, he could picture the scene. Red forms suddenly leaping up from the ditches, from behind the hedges of that sunken, winding lane. Charging the log barricades, their bobbing war-bonnets and paint-daubed faces fearsome to look upon, their high-pitched screaming war whoops hideous to hear . . . charging in suicidal manner and gaining a foothold.

Almost, so clear was that picture in his mind, he could look down into the narrow street and see it filled with naked brown bodies, with the Indians hacking down the white defenders, then fighting street by street right through the town . . .

McGaughey stopped daydreaming. He saw brown bodies out there in the fields. The Indians were moving in.

Already they had skirted past the isolated stone farmhouse. He was seeing what he had imagined only a few seconds before.

His rifle leapt to his shoulder. He fired. Missed. The Indian came crawling along that ditch a few yards further and then disappeared among some rank grasses that betokened water — a seepage hole or perhaps a spring. McGaughey reloaded but was too late for a second shot. He cursed his oldfashioned single-shot Martin. For Indian fighting they needed repeaters.

He had heard that most of these Indians had acquired fine Winchester repeaters, and he prayed that couldn't be entirely true.

Alabastor shouted from the unseen barricade below, 'Who fired that shot?'

McGaughey called down, 'I did — sir. McGaughey.' His eyes narrowed against the bright sunlight, were watching for another creeping form to move within rifle range.

'Can you see anything?'

McGaughey shifted, lifted his gun and took aim. While waiting for his target to reappear, he reported, 'They've flanked that outpost, sir. I can see some braves creeping along a ditch towards the Dutch barn.'

He heard the lieutenant give some orders to the defenders at the barricade. Along to his right, but unseen because of the slope of the roof, he heard two or three guns begin to fire. McGaughey's words had directed other rooftop defenders' attention towards that ditch and now they were concentrating on it.

He lowered his own rifle. The fire was premature. The Indians had gone to ground.

An hour passed, a hot, uncomfortable hour up there on the burning shingles of that cottage roof. Sometimes McGaughey saw Indians, and always they were nearer. His mouth was dry and his eyes ached with staring into the bright sunlight, but he never relaxed his vigilance. His life and the lives of all these white people depended upon men's vigilance, he thought.

About noon, sounds of battle drifted down from the smoke-shrouded north sector of the town. Because of the lack of activity on the west front it made the defenders uneasy, and repeatedly the lieutenant detailed a trooper to go off and find out the situation at the other end of the town. Once McGaughey called down to know what was happening, and the lieutenant himself shouted back a reply.

'There's nothing to worry about yet. The Indians are close to the barricades behind a long ditch and in some houses. But the barricades are strong up there and they think they can hold out.'

McGaughey heard someone down below ask another question, and then the lieutenant's voice, 'Some killed . . . quite a lot wounded.'

Wounded. It made him think of the old doctor. He would be very busy this morning, then. Idly he began to think about Lockland, about that betraying expression which told of the older man's knowledge of McGaughey's past.

Lying up there with the sun hot on his back, staring onto those hedges and gardens that formed an untidy pattern out to the orderly fields beyond his post didn't seem important. It didn't seem of any consequence that anyone should know of it.

And Sara Buie. It wasn't important that she might become embarrassing to a man who had no thought for a serious affair with the girl, who might, because of circumstances, become tied closer to him than he wanted.

All he knew just then was that he was glad she was here so close to him, that she would be on hand when relief came from this fighting.

He kept thinking about her, seeing her pleasant picture before him, and yet at no time did his thoughts come between him and vigilance. The moment a good target showed itself, McGaughey's rifle jarred against his shoulder; he saw a convulsive movement and he knew he had scored a hit. After a time someone crawled up to the prone warrior and began to drag his form under cover.

McGaughey felt pleased with himself. He had shot his first Indian. All his adult life he had taken pleasure in mending men's bodies; now he found some primitive instinct thrilling just as much at hurting an enemy.

He reloaded and waited. He was sure by now that most of those outlying cottages were occupied by Indians. He thought they would be waiting until they were in sufficient force to make an all-out assault on the barricades.

The firing north of them continued in intensity. McGaughey began to believe that the situation there might be more alarming than the lieutenant had told them. With all that firing, it must have been quite a fierce battle, he was sure . . .

The Sioux infantry came surging suddenly out of the nearby cottages at a moment when their cavalry had started to race in across the level fields. Clearly the simultaneous attack was more than a coincidence.

McGaughey saw leaping red forms, just as he had imagined them. Heard blood-chilling war cries and saw hideous daubed faces and bodies. The Sioux were racing in at incredible speed. They weren't bothering about cover.

There must have been fifty or sixty attacking this one spot. Their repeaters were being fired from their hips as they ran in, their bullets spraying the defence works at the end of the street and keeping the defenders crouching and withholding their fire at a critical moment.

Some hidden Sioux were watching for the rooftop defenders and a bullet ripped hard splinters from the shingle almost under McGaughey's face. He fired and saw a Sioux topple. Reloaded. Fired again as the screaming Indian horde reached the barricade. Above the shouting of men he heard the lieutenant's voice.

He had time to think, 'He's a good officer, that Alabastor. He won't run.' And then he fired again and an Indian died right on top of the barricade. McGaughey couldn't see the stacked logs that formed it, but the attacking Indians were in sight of him as they scaled the barricade.

Indians were over the defences. He could hear them fighting savagely in the street below. He stayed where he was, reloading and firing at the Indian reinforcements hurtling towards the breached defences. Alabastor was encouraging the defenders, probably fighting like a demon, McGaughey thought.

He reloaded, fired again. The Indian horsemen were strung out in a long line across the fields, leaping the hedges and heading straight towards the broken barricade. McGaughey's fingers flew as they inserted fresh shells, aimed and fired and reloaded again. At that range he couldn't miss.

There was little firing from the roofs about him; as if the defenders had withdrawn so as not to be cut off now the Indians were in the town. But McGaughey stayed on. He knew he was more effective firing down on to the Indians than in the street with them.

The Indian cavalry was racing in among the cottages now. It was going to be a bad thing for the town if those fierce horsemen leapt the barricade and went rampaging through the streets, McGaughey realised.

They were turning up the sunken lane, that narrow, high-banked winding road that had been so useful to the Sioux infantry in their stealthy advance. McGaughey realised that there was no firing now from that distant outpost. All the defenders must have been killed . . .

His rifle jumped. The Indian chief leading the charge up the sunken lane went flying over the ears of a horse that crumpled dead beneath him. Other ponies ran on to the falling form. There was a crash, screams of pain from tortured, falling horses. In seconds that lane was blocked by a wall of tangled horseflesh and naked Indian riders.

It stopped for vital moments the attack upon the breached defences. McGaughey could see a lane filled with jostling Indian horsemen. He saw attempts to drag the ponies up the steep grassy banks — only to fail time after time.

He saw the confusion; saw Indians turning in their saddles to shout back along the crowded lane. Then the rearmost Indians understood and came circling on to the cultivated land above the lane.

But valuable seconds had been lost to the Indian attack, and now the Sioux cavalry was spread out and was having to pick its way slowly over garden plots and through clinging thin hedges. The attack had failed because of a lucky shot and the circumstances of that sunken, winding lane that was the best approach to these western defences.

The fighting was still ferocious, down in the street below. But now McGaughey heard less of Indian war cries and more savage imprecations from white men. Reinforcements must have been rushed into the street from the centre of the town. Now the Indians, caught over the barricade, were cornered and being shot down.

McGaughey wiped pespiration from his eyes. He found his hand was shaking with excitement. He was realising that if the Indian cavalry could have followed through the gap made by that breaching party, by now the fighting would be many streets deep into the town.

'By God, we were lucky!' he thought, and realisation of their narrow escape brought an exhultation upon him that seemed near to intoxication. He concentrated his fire upon some Indian infantry who were looking back in undecided manner towards the stumbling, slow-moving cavalry.

All at once there was a burst of

cheering from the street below. McGaughey knew then that the Indians had been overpowered, that the white men were manning the defences again. He kept hearing the lieutenant's encouraging voice. Alabastor — he was the man who had turned this battle, McGaughey told himself, crouching behind that ridge and reloading. Alabastor had guts and wouldn't give in and wouldn't let others give in. All the same, it was a pity there weren't more defenders up on the rooftops, with that Indian cavalry no more than fifty yards away and picking their way closer to the defences.

He called down to the lieutenant. 'We need more men on the roofs — sir.' Always he had to think before remembering the 'sir'. 'What's happened to the men who were there before?' But he knew. They had skedaddled, he thought grimly. The faint-hearts had quit.

He heard Alabastor's voice below, driving the men back to their posts. His tone was blistering, threatening. Then the Sioux cavalry were riding right up to the defences.

Perhaps, though, that first minor victory over the Indian infantry had a psychological effect upon both sides. It must have inspired the white defenders, given them a greater hope and courage than they'd had before . . . these Indians weren't superhuman, they could be defeated by resolute men, just as the lieutenant had told them.

And the Indian cavalry were affected equally but in adverse fashion. They had seen their cunning plan upset. The barricade that should have been open to them because of their infantry was now being hastily thrown up again; the defences bristled once more with fierce-eyed white defenders.

Their attack was disjointed. They raged against the barricade, firing their rifles and even trying to leap from their horses on to the defences. But there were too many of them. They got in each other's way. They were easy targets for the palefaces crouching behind their thick protecting barrier of logs.

McGaughey, surprisingly cool and methodical in his movements now, saw those circling, war-bonneted Indians seem to flinch before the deadly discharge of those guns at the barricade. He heard Indian voices shouting, like men uncertain of their next movements and seeking orders.

Then a few at the rear broke away and galloped for the cover of the cottages. The movement spread. The cheering settlers found themselves presented with brown, naked backs for targets. Desperate Sioux warriors were struck down from the rear by those deadly lead missiles; everywhere McGaughey could see them toppling from their saddles or slumping across the necks of their mounts and finding refuge only by clinging to the manes of their wide-eyed, terrified little ponies.

The attack had been beaten off. It

wasn't even safe for the Sioux cavalry to stay behind the cottages, because they were too many and were good targets for the cock-a-hoop defenders. After a few more uncertain minutes the whole troop pulled away westward, to that distant, tree-topped knoll.

There was still steady firing to the north of the town, but in the vicinity of the barricade below McGaughey, the delight of the victorious settlers was almost delirious. He crawled to the edge of the roof and looked down. He was sharing the general satisfaction and knew there was a grin on his face that normally might have irritated him because it would have made him feel ridiculous. But just now relief at having shared in a successful battle made him feel oblivious to appearances.

Women had come flocking into the street, bringing food and drink and fresh ammunition. Men were hugging their wives and daughters for joy, while the blue-shirted cavalry stood back and watched tolerantly — perhaps wishing they had wives to hug at that moment.

But some of the women weren't joyous. Some were crouching over loved ones, weeping in that empty, awful way of women who have lost their men.

McGaughey saw that the fight had been hard, down in the street below. There were many corpses, some naked Indians', others white settlers'. Men were walking among them, examining the bodies and calling when they found life in any of their comrades.

Little parties were putting wounded on to doors and gates and carrying them quickly away towards the centre of the town. McGaughey, curiously, had no feeling at that moment of wanting to go and tend to the wounded. This was reaction to his participation in battle. He felt he wanted to stay up on that roof and see this fight through to the end. His blood was up, he thought, and it made him grin to himself. He had never pictured himself in the role of warrior before.

He stayed where he was, in view of

the men in the street below him. Others were on watch on the rooftops and he knew it was safe enough for him to be away from his post. He wanted to attract attention, to get water held up to him. His thirst was a raging fire now.

Alabastor was standing in a doorway, meat in one hand, a tin cup of water in the other. He was joking with some of the settlers, relaxed, delighted by the victory, enjoying a respite before the next Sioux foray.

Patiently waiting to catch the eye of one of the girls with the water can, McGaughey saw a youth thread his way down the street and approach the lieutenant. Alabastor paused in the act of drinking, listening. Then he nodded.

He looked up and his eyes promptly fell on McGaughey. He jerked his head, an order for McGaughey to come down. The Harvard man promptly slung his rifle, slid over the edge of the cottage, held on to the gutter by his hands and then dropped. He began to go across towards the lieutenant. Some of the wounded were moaning piteously.

As he came close to Alabastor he heard the lieutenant detail another trooper to take McGaughey's place on the roof. McGaughey didn't like the sound of that. It seemed as though his withdrawal from that good vantage point was to be permanent.

Alabastor was in a friendly mood. 'Doctor Lockland's asked if you can be relieved to help him with the wounded. He says he can't cope; there's too many. Better report to him as soon as you've had something to drink, McGaughey.'

Then he added, 'You did well up here, Mac. I wish the others had stuck to their posts like you did.'

McGaughey turned away. There was just a little frown on his forehead, just a faint rebellious feeling inside him. His blood was still up, running hot after that quick, savage battle; he realised that he didn't want to put his gun down, didn't want to shut himself away with a lot of wounded in a whitewashed cellar.

Then he saw a man with a crushed chest being handled badly. His professional instincts returned instantly. McGaughey the soldier vanished; Doctor McGaughey went jumping forward, swearing, instead.

He started to examine the wounded. He did it swiftly, calling upon some of the women to follow him and receive his instructions. One shoved a water-filled tin dipper into his hand and he gulped it all down in an instant and then went on with his work.

He was back at his old job. Don't move that man, just make him comfortable. He was dying and there was no sense in hurrying him out of the world.

Slide that man on to a gate and get him to the hospital; but first a tourniquet to stop that arterial bleeding. This man can walk if supported. This man has had a hefty blow on the head; let him sit in the shade and he'll be all right for the next attack.

And so on. Willing women hung on

to his words and obeyed his instructions. Alabastor was watching, thinking that here was a man efficient at his job. Within minutes there was order among the wounded where before had been panic and uncertainty . . .

A settler, about to go into a house for some reason or other, shouted an alarm. Every head there turned. He was standing in an open doorway, pointing inside. Suddenly he jumped sideways back into the street. An Indian axe fell weakly where he had been standing.

Men slipped off the safety catches of their rifles and went plunging towards the door. McGaughey had been looking at a man with a broken back, a man who had been shot from a rooftop and was in a bad way. He was quite near the doorway.

In the rush towards the open door he found himself being carried forward; without wanting to, found himself first to look into that plainly-furnished settlers' home.

He saw two Indians in the shadows

to the rear. Both were wounded, he saw at a glance. Both were in a bad way. There was blood all over the floor, showing where they had dragged themselves out of the fight.

One Indian, clad in buckskin trousers only, seemed almost unconscious, his eyes barely open. He was lying in the arms of a younger man, a man who snarled defiance, as a wolf does when found after days in a cruel trap. He had a knife held threatening aloft, and yet McGaughey could see the trembling that told of weakness. He was losing a lot of blood from a great gaping hole just above his thigh bone.

McGaughey heard the roar of vengeance break from those bearded settlers' throats as they saw two enemies, helpless before them. Men tried to crash past him, to be first to administer the death blows to these Indians. He heard gun hammers click back, knew that shots would be fired any instant.

McGaughey found himself throwing

back the settlers. At first it was almost an unconscious action, but immediately it became more than that. He found himself turning, pushing back those men in the doorway, shouting to them.

He was a doctor again. It went against his instincts to see wounded men killed. An injury was a challenge to his experience; he had to exert his skill to repair the damage.

He found himself shouting, 'Goldarn it, they can't do any harm. Let 'em live!'

It wasn't a popular sentiment, but his voice carried authority in it. Those men found themselves losing their anger, their hatred. They found themselves obeying automatically, even though afterwards they growled and wondered because they had done so.

McGaughey turned. He found himself panting from the exertion. In this airless room he felt stifled. He saw those glittering eyes in the gloom at the back of the room and walked towards the Indians. He carried no arms in his hands; his rifle was still slung across his back.

The Indian raised his knife a little higher, a little more threatening. His breath was coming in quick, convulsive gasps. McGaughey was no fool and didn't walk on to that blade. Instead he moved swiftly to one side, just as swiftly came back, caught the wrist of that Indian before the warrior quite knew what was happening.

The grip was weak. McGaughey took the knife without difficulty. Then the whole body of the young brave relaxed, his head drooped.

9

McGaughey pulled the older, heavier warrior out of the younger man's arms. They were probably father and son, he thought. The older man stirred and moaned, and McGaughey bent over to examine him first. It was hard to see.

He turned, saw the silent, hostile crowd in the doorway, and shouted, 'Give me light. Stand back there!'

The crowd began to move away sullenly. Curiously, they all went. Quite unexpectedly, McGaughey found himself alone with the Indians. He looked at the young warrior, lying in a pool of blood, watching him with savage brown eyes.

Then he shrugged. He wasn't going to call any of that crowd back to watch over his patients.

He set to work on the older Indian. He was bleeding from a jagged wound in the neck. It was from a severed artery, and McGaughey could see that he was almost dead from loss of blood. He tore off a strip of buckskin, wrapped a small stone that had been kicked inside the door in the folds, and then applied it to the wound. After a few seconds he felt satisfied that the bleeding would stop and he turned to the younger warrior.

This time, the brave let him examine his wound between the ribs and the thigh bone. When he gently turned the warrior over he saw a hole at the back, too. Someone had clapped a gun against the man's side and fired from point blank range, he decided from the powder-charred flesh.

He looked into the young warrior's eyes. There was no hostility in them now. Only fear. McGaughey knew what that fear was; he had seen it many times on the faces of his white patients. It was the fear of death. When the time came, nobody wanted to die. Now that young warrior was suddenly trusting him, placing his life in McGaughey's hands. Doing it because he had to, because there was no seeming alternative, yet doing it willingly.

He let McGaughey examine the wound, let him pull him close to the light while he probed with a knife point to make sure there was no piece of bullet with the splintered bone. Then McGaughey bandaged him in a way as to stop the bleeding.

A few people had drifted back by now, fascinated by the sight of their formidable enemies. McGaughey heard them talking, growling among themselves. The sojer was wasting his time on those varmints when there were white men to attend to, one belligerent-voiced settler kept saying.

McGaughey hadn't thought of it that way. He had gone instinctively to attend to these wounded, Indians though they were, because they had been the nearest in need of him. That was all.

But as he stood up, glad to get the kink out of his knees, he realised that if he took his eyes off these Indians for long, he would have been wasting his time in attending to them. The thought made him obstinate. These weren't enemies any longer. A little while ago he had been shooting to kill Indians, would have shot these if they had come up level with his sights. But that had been in defence of his own life. They weren't enemies now. They were his patients.

He looked at the doorway, becoming more and more crowded. They were a hostile lot standing there. Some women were among them. They were sharing the hostility of their menfolk, but McGaughey knew how to get them round to his side.

He touched the black hair of the younger warrior. He was watching those women. 'He's only a boy,' he said. He repeated it: 'A boy. He was trying to help his father, and risked his life in the process.'

He saw the expressions change on those women's faces. He had known it would happen. He pointed to one of them, young, no older than himself, a wife and mother he guessed.

'You take charge of him. Him and his father. Get some men to carry them along with our wounded to the schoolhouse. I hold you responsible.'

He pushed his way through the little crowd at that, as the woman and some of her friends went into the room. He knew they wouldn't let anyone kill the Indians under their eyes; knew no man would cold-bloodedly kill them while those women were there. It was queer, but that was how men and women behaved before each other, he knew.

The Indians were brought by stretcher parties to the schoolhouse less then ten minutes later. McGaughey was with the doctor. There were wounded sitting outside on the schoolhouse wall, silent, ill-looking men in improvised bloody bandages. The ground floor of the schoolhouse was like a charnel house.

Here were the worst wounded, the

most seriously afflicted and dying. Looking upon those dozens of wounded, McGaughey was momentarily horrified. Then he threw away the feeling that this job was too big for two men to tackle. He sought out the little, grey-haired doctor.

The man was doing his best, but he was overwhelmed. There was too much for him, too much for any one man. And people were pushing their wounds before him, demanding priority. There was too much shouting, too much hysteria, McGaughey decided. Order, that was what was needed.

The little doctor found himself being lifted from beside a patient whose chest was being bandaged. McGaughey pointed to a woman who was carrying water for the doctor. 'That's a job you can finish for the doctor,' he said peremptorily. Then he faced that circle of pressing wounded. His eyes flashed with anger.

'Get back, you!' he thundered. 'Go on, get right outside this building. The people who need first attention are those who can't come shoving their scratches under the doctor's nose.'

A bewildered Doctor Lockland saw the tall young trooper drive the least wounded through the schoolhouse door. They were shouting, protesting, getting panicky and angry with McGaughey. He shouted them down and drove them all out.

The schoolroom seemed blessedly peaceful after that.

McGaughey saw a few women trying to attend to some prostrate, groaning men on the floor. He snapped, 'Doctor, examine those men first. Don't do any bandaging. Pick intelligent women to follow you; tell 'em what to do and leave it to them. There's no time to linger over any one patient.'

He was like a cyclone in that schoolhouse, a blue cyclone some of the women were thinking. They were watching the trooper almost fearfully, scared to turn those cold grey eyes upon themselves. But they had to admit that he had secured order in a matter of minutes, something the old doctor hadn't done in hours. And they had been frightened by all the shouting and pushing, by the near-hysteria of some of the selfish wounded.

McGaughey went down into the cellar ward. All the beds were occupied, but most of the wounded could be taken elsewhere, he decided. If they were to use that adjoining room as an operating theatre they would have need of these beds for the seriously wounded. A woman had followed him down the stairs. He gave an order: 'Get him and him' — he began to indicate — 'in beds elsewhere. Ask householders to take them in. They're not too badly hurt.'

Then he discovered that the woman was Sara.

He paused, smiled, then went three at a time up the steps. Later he saw Sara taking women below to help move the lightly injured.

When he showed in the school

doorway a clamour of sound greeted him. He ignored it and began walking out among the wounded. He saw a man with his foot dangling. The ankle had been smashed at close range by a bullet. The man was white and unconscious. Here was a man who needed immediate attention and not these other walking wounded.

He called for able-bodied men to get the man down below; shouted to the women to put him to bed. When there was time he would examine and operate where required.

He picked out the worst hurt. Then the two Indians were carried in. He ordered them to be put on mattresses in a corner of the schoolroom where he could keep an eye on them. He didn't trust some of those vengeful whites. The younger Indian watched the activity all about him but never said a word, never changed that expression of fear and murder. McGaughey had to remember he might be thirsty and despatched a girl with water for the Indians . . . the young brave seemed as much afraid of the girl as she was of her unusual patients.

With the worst wounded down below, McGaughey began to pick out those who could best do with Doctor Lockland's attentions. He got them lined up inside the door, threatening that if any man tried to get priority he would go right to the back of the queue. It worked. There was no trouble after that.

But always more wounded were being carried up or came walking in. There was still steady fighting to the north of the town, and inevitably, in spite of the thick barriers behind which they fought, settlers got hurt. Mostly they were head injuries, many of them beyond McGaughey's powers as a surgeon.

He saw Sara. He called to her and she came running. There was no smiles between them now. They were doctor and assistant, and the work on hand was too serious for any softer distraction of their thoughts.

McGaughey said, 'Sara, we need ten times this room for wounded. Go round the houses, find spare beds and arrange for the wounded to be taken in and looked after. That's your job from now on.'

He turned his attention to the wounded, satisfied that Sara would handle the situation capably and intelligently. That was the way it should be done, he thought; get other people to do the work — do only that work himself that no others could do.

He went below, into the operating room.

* * *

The Sioux came storming back at that western barricade later that afternoon. First a stealthy, almost undetected advance by Sioux infantry. Then a simultaneous attack by cavalry and infantry. This time, though, the Sioux avoided using that sunken lane which was at once the most convenient approach to the barricaded street and a potential death trap. They came across open country, and clearly they had learned the quickest approaches from their first advance.

This attack was more formidable than the first. Where hundreds had been in that first assault, now there were thousands massing to try to storm the western defences.

At the same time, an all-out assault was set up at several other points around the town, doubtless to prevent reserves from being hurried to the most desperately attacked spot, the western side . . . Flagstaff's most vulnerable position because of those outbuildings that gave protection to advancing infantry. Now men understood why Alabastor had placed himself and his trained soldiers there.

All during the hot day, with the crackle of gunfire raging around them, McGaughey and the little doctor strove to cope with the procession of wounded that came from the barricades for their attention. McGaughey was operating, using courageous women as nurses to help him. Lockland was now diagnosing, directing the worst wounded down to McGaughey and attending to the others himself.

It was a hectic time, a seeming confusion of activity among those groaning, bleeding people. But McGaughey felt satisfied they had the work organised as well as it was humanly possible.

Then, with the coming of darkness, the attack lessened and finally petered away. By some miracle the settlers had managed to hold their barricades. It had cost them dearly, however. Looking at that army of injured, quite apart from their many dead, McGaughey couldn't help wondering how they would manage to stem off the next assault.

If there was another assault, that was. The Sioux might now have decided that attacking towns wasn't worthwhile and might depart in the night for easier victories. But McGaughey felt they would be out across those fields in the morning, gathering their strength for another attack.

Lamps were lit. The evening was warm and fine and when he had performed his last operation, McGaughey was glad to come out into the square away from the heady odour of ether. He took food and drink, looking at the patient queues of wounded still waiting for attention. Doctor Lockland was moving among them, working in the open lamplight.

Sara came up to him. She must have been keeping watch for him. She looked tired but cheerful. Now they could afford to smile at each other.

'That was hectic.'

'It was awful.' He put down his coffee, smiling and thinking how fine she looked. Not just pretty, though; she had courage and there was intelligence on her face. A good girl, Sara Buie.

Buie? He deferred the question that came leaping into his mind.

'You were . . . wonderful,' she said impulsively. There were lights in her eyes. Was it admiration or adoration? Hero worship. He liked it, whatever it was, but of course couldn't show it.

'The whole town's talking about you. Doctor Lockland says you've done more than anyone to save the town.' That was generous of the older doctor, but many others were more deserving of the praise. Alabastor for one, he thought. 'He says if you hadn't stopped the beginnings of panic among the wounded there's no knowing how it would have affected the defences.'

'Doctor Lockland has done as much,' he told her. 'There was just too much for one man, and he was tired to begin with.'

She was smiling at him, shaking her head. 'No one in the town will believe that. There isn't a man or woman here who doesn't swear by you; who wouldn't ask for you if they were seriously hurt. You've done a wonderful job here today — '

' — Jim.'

'Jim,' she smiled. Doctor Lockland was standing near, looking up from a head wound he was cleaning. 'The whole town is asking why you're in the ranks instead of doctoring.'

McGaughey looked at Lockland. Found himself saying, 'I think Doctor Lockland understands.' The two doctors' eyes met, then Lockland looked away.

Alabastor came in from the barricades for a rest. He was grimy, weary but cheerful. He sought out the trooper working under the lamplight outside the schoolhouse.

'Hello, there, Mac.' There was that friendly greeting again. 'Everyone's telling me you've done a magnificent piece of work here.'

McGaughey looked up. The praise was genuine and he felt slightly embarrassed. 'It had to be done. I was trained in this work.' He shrugged.

Alabastor gulped coffee. It was hot and he made a noise about it. He said, 'I've had a request from the town's leaders for you to remain at your doctoring. I think you're more use here than with a gun in your hand.'

McGaughey found himself laughing, remembering. 'I'm not sure I'm pleased about that — sir. I found myself enjoying that first attack. It was a new experience, I suppose. Even now it sounds more thrilling than cutting out bullets and strapping up broken limbs.'

Quite a fire-eater, eh?' The two laughed at each other. It was curious that only a couple of days before, there had been a stiffness about their conversation, a suspicion on the part of the lieutenant that the Harvard man was vaguely too free in his manner towards authority. Now they were comrades and friends.

'You'll have to stay as doctor, Mac. Sorry.' He didn't sound sorry. 'If I take you away I think the whole town will mutiny!'

Again they laughed. Interested, Alabastor followed McGaughey round and watched while he attended the last of the wounded. Then he said he would have to go.

'Back on watch, sir?' McGaughey looked up.

'Not on watch. I'm taking a party to fire those outbuildings. The settlers have given permission. There's no opposition now. They realise that the western approaches are the most dangerous for us. If we clear the ground, the damned Indian infantry won't be able to come sneaking right up to our barricade.'

McGaughey walked away with him. 'What are our chances, even so?'

Alabastor shrugged. 'If they concentrate their attack, as they should have done today, they could be all over the town within half an hour of sunrise. But that's not the Indian way of fighting. Every man's an individual. You don't get them fighting together.'

'There were signs of planning earlier

today, though.' McGaughey was thinking of the timing of that first Indian cavalry attack the moment the infantry surged forward to breach the defences.

'Yes, there's someone with a tactical mind. He's the man I'm scared of. In time they'll be listening to him, following his ideas. Then — '

'Then I'll drop my surgeon's knife and pick up my gun again!'

Alabastor laughed.

'Well, good luck, sir. Don't run into trouble out there.'

'Indians aren't much trouble after dark.'

That's what they all said, McGaughey thought. He wasn't so sure. He watched Alabastor stride away into the darkness. That young officer had the right spirit. More of him down at Richmond instead of officers who had secured commissions by influence and not by merit and the Union forces wouldn't now be reeling in defeat.

He went back to the schoolhouse, musing on the turn of events. Who would have thought that an Indian war would have developed while civil war was raging over the land . . .

He suddenly noticed how people gave way respectfully before him. They fell back at his approach, but did it with a smile on their faces. Men and women, the injured and their attendants, were all deferring to him, he realised.

He felt his blood tingling. It was good to have earned their respect. He liked it — what man wouldn't. And it brought his head higher with pride, put a jauntiness back into his tired step.

His eyes fell on the two Indians just inside the schoolroom on their mattresses. He went to them to attend their wounds.

'Are they getting food and drink?' he called to some of the women on duty in the schoolroom. They weren't sure.

'See that they get the same treatment as our wounded,' he ordered. He knew now that no more harm would come to the wounded enemy. He, Trooper McGaughey, had ordered it; he, Doctor

McGaughey, was all-important to the community now and his orders weren't to be flouted.

The older Indian was stronger, but still his eyes were partly closed from weakness. He made no sound as McGaughey put a fresh bandage on and made him more comfortable. The bleeding started again but McGaughey knew it would soon stop.

Then he went to the younger warrior. He must have been in great pain, and McGaughey wished that he had drugs to deaden it but he hadn't. As he attended to the ugly wound the Indian kept withdrawing, flinching. McGaughey kept saying, 'I can't help it, brother. You've got to stand this pain if you're going to get better. Think twice next time you take to war.'

But he knew what had brought them on to the war trails they had forsworn. Hunger. They weren't altogether to blame.

He found Sara following him.

'You're tired, Sara.'

'No tireder than you.' That quick smile, embracing him in its warmth.

'All the same, it's time you found a bed.' He put his arm across her shoulders and steered her to the door. There she stopped.

'I haven't a bed in this town. I've nowhere to go.' But she didn't sound bothered. She was lucky to be alive and she knew it.

McGaughey was tired. He felt it suddenly and eased himself down on the schoolhouse step. Sara sat beside him, neatly, dress pulled down so that only the tips of her worn shoes showed, her hands clasped on her lap.

He had a feeling of content and wondered how much of it was due to the presence of this girl by his side. It couldn't all be satisfaction because of a good day's work done.

He looked round, then began to fumble for his pipe. He smoked little, but now it seemed necessary to complete his feeling of well-being and tired ease.

The yellow lamps, swinging under the trees, besieged by swarms of insects, made mellow the scene around him. He saw the rows of wounded, lying on their mattresses or blankets for fifty yards on either side of the schoolhouse. Mostly they were sleeping now, though a few groaned in the grip of an agony that seemed too much for them to endure. Yet these weren't the worst cases.

He looked beyond the trees that shaded the square saw the silhouettes of houses against a sky that was paling as a moon began to rise. He thought, 'Alabastor must be quick.' Moonlight might be revealing, dangerous.

'Sara.' She looked up. He was puffing at his pipe. 'I saw your name in a Gin County news-sheet a few days ago.'

Her hands seemed to tighten upon themselves. McGaughey found himself wishing he had read that account more carefully.

'It's been in quite a lot lately,' she said dully, not looking at him. So that lynching concerned her family. Buie wasn't a common name and he hadn't much doubt about it from the first.

McGaughey said with assurance, 'It's got something to do with these attacks upon you and your brother.'

Sara turned to him, and there was pain and bewilderment on her face. 'That's what I keep thinking, but, Jim it isn't understandable. Whatever people said, my father wasn't a Confederate sympathiser. It wasn't true that he approved of slavery and was against the Union.'

She was talking now, telling him what he wanted to know. In defence of his curiosity he thought, 'They attacked me as well. I should know what it's all about.'

They sat in the warmth of the night on that schoolhouse step, the wounded all about them, while she talked.

'My father was outspoken. He wouldn't keep to himself unpopular thoughts, and for that reason he didn't have many friends. But he meant well, my father.' There were tears in her eyes.

'He worked hard and did everything for his children that a father should. Only, ever since mother's death a few years back, he didn't seem to care about people or their opinions.

'When John Brown made his attack on slave owners at Harper's Ferry my father called him a murderous old madman who would bring his country into war. At a time when Northern sympathisers were making a martyr of John Brown you can imagine how unpopular my father's sentiments were.'

'You think your father was right?'

'I do.' She was quite vigorous about it. 'You see, my father believed that war would be more terrible than the slavery that existed in a few states. He said war solved nothing — '

'He was right there.'

His tone encouraged her. She hadn't been sure he would be understanding.

'He talked against war but people persisted in believing that he talked against the Union. Oh, it is so easy for people to misunderstand!' Sara said bitterly. 'We knew what it was to be insulted in the stores and street, but we knew our father was right and we tried not to feel anger towards our persecutors.

'That was why Frank, my brother, wanted so badly to join the Union forces. He was as much opposed as anyone to slavery. If his country was at war, then he felt he must play his part in it to help get rid of slavery.'

'But what happened?' He saw the little look of surprise on her face. 'I mean, to your father? I only glanced at that paper.'

'They hanged him and then fired our farmhouse,' she said. The tears were falling but her grief was silent.

'Who hanged him?' He hated to question her, but so far he had learned little.

'I don't know. That's the trouble. What does it matter, anyway?'

'But it might matter.' He put his hand over hers on her lap. 'Come, Sara. Hold up; try to tell me everything. It isn't a nice thought to feel that someone has wanted to kill anyone as sweet as you.'

He got a smile for that, a quick flashing smile that lit up her face. She did take hold of herself and spoke more calmly after that.

'It was one afternoon. I was in town and Frank was working on a neighbour's land. Suddenly the neighbour's wife came running down to him shouting that it looked as if our farmhouse was on fire.

'Frank started to run for home as hard as he could, when he came out on to the back lane he could see rising smoke and he knew our home was on fire. As he climbed up the hill he ran into some soldiers. They shouted to him to keep out of the way; there was a lynching party down at the farm and he had better hide until they'd gone. Frank said they were running as if scared themselves. Lynchers don't like being watched, he said.'

She paused, thinking into a past that

was painful. Then she went on: 'Frank didn't stop, of course. But he found those men had been right. A lynching party had been down at the farm. Daddy . . . was hanging from a tree outside our house. And the house . . . '

'Was a blazing ruin.' McGaughey had imagination. He could picture the scene, could imagine the boy's horror and later the girl's. It was a bad way for life to end, for a man's children to see him like that. 'And the lynching party?'

'They weren't there. They must have run away at sight of Frank — or perhaps those soldiers had scared them.'

'You don't know who those lynchers were?'

Old Lockland came and sat with them. Sara spoke on without restraint at his presence. He was a friendly, harmless old man and quite probably had heard the full story, anyway.

'Tom Henderson, the marshal, came out a few times to look at the burnt farm, but he never seemed to get any nearer identifying the miscreants, either. He came and questioned us a lot when we moved to that little cottage outside Gin Point.'

Doctor Lockland came into the conversation. 'I know Tom. Big and slow-looking, but he has brains. He'd find the lynchers if anyone could.' He had produced a pipe. McGaughey gave him his tobacco and the two doctors smoked for a while in silence.

Then McGaughey said, 'Nothing dovetails. That's the most unsatisfying story I've heard for a long time, Sara, and I can't tell you why.'

The girl looked at him, her brow puckering slightly, as if not understanding. There seemed some sort of noise beginning east of the town. It was nothing as yet but they were all listening even while McGaughey spoke.

'There hadn't been any other lynchings in Gin County?'

'Not for months . . . probably over a year. Just a little after the declaration of war against the South,' Doctor Lockland answered. The old man seemed interested in this conversation.

'Then why suddenly this hanging? Lynchers aren't brave men, either. Usually it takes a few dozen of 'em to get up courage to string a man. When so many people become involved it isn't long before a whisper gets around and everyone knows who's in it. A smart man like Tom Henderson would have known the lynchers within days. No, Sara, you've told me half the story so far — '

'I've told you all I know.'

'Sure.' McGaughey smiled and patted her hand. 'But you've still told me half the story. The rest is for someone . . . Tom Henderson, maybe . . . to find out.'

Lockland was watching the younger man. He respected McGaughey's intelligence, and now he pondered on what he had heard and tried to see what the Harvard man saw in it.

They all looked up. McGaughey exclaimed, 'Now, what's that noise about?'

Behind the schoolhouse, on the east road out, there was a rising hum of excitement, the noise of many people gathered together. Then it seemed to the people in that square that with it was mingled something like a cheer.

McGaughey relaxed back on the doorstep and puffed again at his pipe. 'Whatever it is, it doesn't seem threatening. And I'm too tired to find out.'

He looked at the doctor.

'You live hereabouts?'

'Near.' The doctor nodded. 'Inside the town. Why?'

'Sara — Sara Buie, as you've probably guessed — needs a bed to sleep on tonight. I'm thinking Doctor Lockland might be able to offer her accommodation while she's within Flagstaff,' the trooper smiled.

'I think so.' Doctor Lockland looked quizzically at the girl. 'If she's a friend of yours — '

Deliberately McGaughey took the

pipe out of his mouth and said, 'Sometimes I've been known to call her my gal.' He grinned at her. 'If we're not careful she'll be finding herself my gal, too.'

Momentarily Sara was taken aback by his frankness; then she found a retort. 'Don't take him too seriously, doctor. Only a couple of days or so ago he was telling a sentry that I'd been drinking too much in Gin Point.'

They were still laughing when the noise crescended abruptly. There was movement across the lamplit square. The wounded tried to sit up on their mattresses, women came crowding behind Sara and the doctors on the step. The disturbance in the night wasn't alarming, but all the same everyone had to know the cause of it — and how it affected their prospect of survival.

The three were standing now, and were peering into the shadows across the square. There was a lot of movement. They began to distinguish forms; saw there were horses . . . horse-men.

Sara gripped McGaughey by the arm. 'Soldiers,' he heard her exclaim. The word was taken up by the wounded and the women about them. The excitement blazed up.

Soldiers. Troopers riding in on jaded horses. The cavalry!

'They've got through! The cavalry made it!'

There were cheers springing to the lips of those delighted people. They were beginning to think, 'We're saved. Now we've nothing to fear from the Sioux.' And then they noticed something.

There weren't many cavalry there, after all. Not enough to guarantee safety . . .

10

The cavalry had come to a halt, strung out across the square. McGaughey was trying to count, peering towards those shadowy figures.

'One company,' he said sullenly, and there was disappointment in his voice. The cheering had subsided. 'Darn it, they've sent one company of cavalry to protect a town from the Sioux!'

The wounded went back on their beds, their gladness, that sudden thrilling moment, dissipating as quickly as it had come. The women went silently back to the bedsides of their patients. One hundred men. That made little or no difference against the might of the Sioux.

McGaughey heard shouted commands and recognised some of the voices. One in particular he knew. It was harsh, angry-sounding, menace and threat carried in every syllable.

The captain. His captain. He had to think to remember his name, though he could picture that heavy, angry face immediately. Hiss. Captain Berkely Hiss. And Surgeon Ned Hiss was his brother.

He saw Lockland trying to stifle a yawn.

'You'd better get off to bed, you two,' he said, and his words sounded like an order. They did protest, all the same. 'We don't all need to stay awake,' he told them. 'You get some sleep — and sleep better for knowing we've got a hundred more men to defend that town tomorrow!'

When he was alone he sat sucking his empty pipe, watching the indistinct movement across the square. He could tell what was happening by the familiar sounds. The clanging of the pump . . . the troopers were getting water for their horses. The rattle of a bailer in a can — that would be water being brought out to the men.

Men's voices, swelling into a steady hum of sound as they relaxed the tension of hours. He knew when food was brought out to them because of the rush of stamping feet and the minor cheer. And then he got the odour of coffee.

He was drowsing now, unheeding the noise and the moaning of the wounded. The yellow lamplight was soothing; he found he wanted to sleep.

Someone shook him. He had been asleep, perhaps for a few minutes only. A trooper was standing over him. He remembered the man; they had shared the same hut at Gin Barracks. And the men remembered McGaughey.

'Wake up, College Boy. The captain wants to know where Lootenant Al-i-bastor is.'

'Ali?' McGaughey rubbed his eyes. Oh, he was tired! Those few minutes' sleep had done him no good at all, had merely served to remind him that he was in need of rest. 'He's out of the town, firing some houses that's in the way of the defence.'

He was pointing towards the west road out. Then he noticed a yellowness over the houses before him. They seemed in stronger silhouette. And then he realised that the light was swiftly brightening, was growing redder.

'That's Alabastor,' he said, nodding. 'Looks like he's got down to work.'

The trooper was turning. Then both heard the swift rattle of distant gunfire, the first since darkness had fallen on the town. McGaughey thought, 'Alabastor's been caught out there.' But there was nothing anyone could do about it. That was a risk Alabastor had knowingly taken in going out with his firing party.

The trooper was weary. 'If Ali comes back, tell him the captain wants to see him right away. And he's in a temper, mean as hell. It's played on his nerves, this last ride into the town.'

'You got in without meeting any Sioux?'

'Never saw a feather. Not after we

struck the plain. While we were in the hills we could see firing. Then we saw the Sioux pull out of battle, and it seemed to us they were all heading across the river before dark. So we took a chance and rode in.'

'They should have sent a regiment not a company. That's what we need.'

'There's another war on. It took them all their time to send us north.'

The trooper's voice was tired. They must have forced-marched to have come so swiftly after receipt of the lieutenant's report. He began to go back across the square.

McGaughey called after him, 'You look like you need some sleep.' He was puzzled. He had just noticed that those shadowy troopers weren't putting up tents under the trees or getting down to sleep in their blankets.

'Sleep?' The trooper halted, peering back at the man sitting on the schoolhouse step, yellow lamplight on his head and shoulders. 'There'll be little sleep for anyone tonight if the captain gets his way.' McGaughey took the pipe out of his mouth. 'He says he won't stop in this town. He says it hasn't a chance tomorrow.' His arm waved vaguely. 'My God, you should have seen what we saw up in the hills. Thousands of 'em, an' more coming up. The captain's right in saying we should all get away in the dark.'

Then he went. McGaughey looked at his empty pipe then turned to look into the schoolroom. If the town was evacuated, the wounded couldn't go with the townspeople. They'd have to be left.

McGaughey looked at his pipe with distaste, then put it away. His head drooped. In a few seconds he was sleeping again, propped against the schoolhouse doorway. Inside, the young Indian, his eyes fever bright, watched him. Sometimes he talked softly to himself, and once he essayed to crawl off his mattress, but the pain came up and hit him and stretched him moaning on his back, his eyes rolling, the whites showing, until the agony subsided a little.

When McGaughey next wakened there were people standing before him. A group of about a dozen men. Two or three were wearing crude, blood-soaked bandages. The others were supporting them and carrying a man on a gate.

McGaughey shoved himself upright, then went across to that man on the improvised stretcher. When he stood over him he said, gently, 'So you didn't keep out of trouble, lootenant?'

Alabastor's face was waxy pale. He tried to smile, but it wasn't a ghost of an effort. McGaughey heard him say, 'Sorry . . . more work for you, Mac.'

The trooper gently pulled back the soaked bandages. Alabastor's arm was smashed below the shoulder. McGaughey frowned when he saw that the penetration had been outside; it raised the problem of where the bullet had lodged itself. His exploring fingers got the answer. It had gone through Alabastor's arm and had smashed into the lieutenant's chest. It couldn't be far from the officer's heart.

'Take him below,' he ordered. Into the small, ether-stinking room. Alabastor was going to need some considerable operation.

He looked swiftly at the wounds of the other men. Not serious, he told them. Painful and exhausting, but they would live. He made jokes about it, but the jokes failed when he thought of the lieutenant's chances.

Some women came up from the darkness. They were always there when he needed them, he thought. Far better than men for this sort of work. He gave quick instructions while Alabastor was carried carefully downstairs.

Then he asked what had happened, and a lean, bullet-headed trooper, who had ridden by McGaughey's side most of the way north, told what had happened.

'We got out. The lootenant crept ahead, makin' sure there wasn't no darned Injuns sleepin' in them cottages.

But there wasn't. So we dragged up straw an' anythin' that looked like it would take flame and the lootenant sent us back while he started the fire.'

The man spat. He was very laconic about the incident, a man who rarely showed emotion. Perhaps, thought McGaughey, he hadn't the imagination to realise how near to death he had been out there.

'Injuns don't sleep in houses — they sleep outside. We should have remembered that. The moment the blaze started, they began to shoot from some way below us. We saw the lootenant go down. That damned cottage went up quicker than we wanted now, and there was so much light all of a sudden it felt like daylight. A few of us rushed back, grabbed the lootenant and dragged him behind the barricade. We stopped lead while doing that.'

They'd gone back. Some of his comrades weren't as gutless as their grousing had suggested, he thought.

Then he thought, 'The expedition

failed. Those buildings are still there to help the Sioux tomorrow morning.' Maybe it would be wiser to evacuate the town while the way east was unwatched.

He went down to his patient.

When he was below he remembered that Captain Hiss wanted the lieutenant. He called a trooper and gave him a message for the captain. 'Tell him the lootenant's got it bad. He won't be doing any visiting for some time.'

Alabastor had been placed on the crude table he used for operations. Two women, without instructions, had come from somewhere and were cutting away his shirt. McGaughey watched them. They were adaptable, these women. They had never done this kind of work before, but today they had done it without flinching.

He looked at the ether bottle against the lamplight. There was very little left. Then he saw the nearly closed eyes resting on him and he went across to the patient.

'You're lucky, lootenant.' He spoke cheerfully. Alabastor would have need of all his courage this night. 'Next crock that comes down these stairs won't have anesthetic to help him.'

He saw that smile on the lieutenant's face. He leaned over him, waiting until the women had cut away the last of the bandages.

'Any objections to a trooper digging into your ribs for a stray bullet, lootenant?'

'Not if it's you, Mac.'

Alabastor meant it. He had seen McGaughey at work and was satisfied. Then he got the sponge for the last precious drops of ether . . .

There was a heavy tramping of feet overhead. They began to stamp down the wooden stairs. There was no attempt at softening the tread, McGaughey noticed, and already it had disturbed some of the uneasy-sleeping wounded.

He went to the door and began to shout, 'Stop that noise. Blast it, this is a hospital . . . '

He stopped. Captain Berkely Hiss was coming down the stairs. Big, hulking Hiss, his face blotched and puffy from the rigours of the trail, his face its usual angry red.

Hiss was glaring at the trooper as if he meant murder. He shouted, 'Is that the way to talk to an officer? Stand to attention!'

McGaughey sighed. Then he stood erect, but it was a parody of attention.

Behind the captain was a retinue of officers and N.C.O.s. A whole string of them peering into the lamplight from that stairway. Somewhere among them was Captain Berkeley Hiss's brother, the regimental surgeon. Everyone looked hostilely at the trooper.

Captain Hiss rapped, 'Where's Lieutenant Alabastor?'

McGaughey was getting tired of that voice but he indicated the operating room. Hiss went in noisily and everyone else followed. McGaughey stood outside and looked at a young woman who was taking water to the patients who were awake. She lifted her eyebrows and McGaughey shrugged.

Then everyone inside the little room started calling for him. He found the two Hiss brothers standing by Alabastor's head. The surgeon was just standing, looking at the exposed wound of the lieutenant, but making no attempt to touch it. His expression was vacuous, his heavy, dough-like face not showing any emotion.

His brother made up for it. He was all emotion, all anger. 'Where's the doctor in charge?'

'In bed — sir.'

Everyone stared at him.

'In bed? But who's looking after Lieutenant Alabastor?' Captain Hiss's words were almost shouted, his eyes protruding with that ever-present anger.

McGaughey sighed. Now for it. 'Me. I am — sir. I was just going to take the ball out of his ribs.'

A moments silence, then Captain Hiss let himself go. He was in the army as a trooper, not as a doctor. By god, it was assault, for a trooper to touch an officer. He must not act as a doctor any more, otherwise . . . And Captain Hiss didn't leave much to his imagination with that threat.

When the captain had subsided a little, McGaughey heard what he had expected. Brother Ned would attend to the lieutenant. McGaughey was watching Alabastor's white face. He saw the eyelids flicker when Captain Hiss said his brother would operate. They opened and looked at McGaughey. McGaughey shrugged. There wasn't anything he could do about it. Alabastor seemed to shiver and then his eyes closed again. There wasn't anything he could do about it, either. Captain Hiss was in charge, and he certainly wouldn't let any trooper be preferred to his brother.

McGaughey watched them both closely. It was interesting to see how Berkely Hiss pushed his brother, helping him all the time, while Brother Ned, slow-moving, turning his head almost with the stiffness of a doll, did as he was told.

Decay. The word came into the Harvard doctor's mind every time he looked at the surgeon. Here was a man mentally even more than physically running downhill. His lips set tight as he thought of him attending to this messy wound of the lieutenant.

He began to go out. Captain Hiss called him back. 'You can help my brother,' rapped the red-faced captain. Hiss began to stamp out of the room. He was talking, giving orders all the way.

Find the darned mayor. See how far he had got into talking the people into leaving the town. Get everyone out. Get the town evacuated within an hour. Parade all the wagons and livestock in the square. Speed, speed. They must get three or four hours' lead, must be ten miles into the hills before the Sioux got on their track.

A sergeant went out last. He was a tired and fed-up man. McGaughey caught his eye and heard the man growl, 'An' if we don't run into a relief column mighty quick, even that ten miles won't do us no good.'

McGaughey picked up the ether sponge. There were lines on his forehead. If there was a relief column (it sounded like slow-moving infantry) somewhere behind Captain Hiss's cavalry, why evacuate the town? They wouldn't stand a chance if the townspeople were caught by the savage Sioux out in the open. Then he shrugged. Captain Berkely Hiss was in charge, and Captain Hiss had decided to pull out.

* * *

He put the ether sponge close to the patient's face, saw Lt. Alabastor struggle and choke and then quickly go limp. He looked up. The surgeon was opening a snuff box. With agonisingly slow movements he took a pinch, sniffed and sneezed and wiped his nostrils with the back of his hand. The snuff fell on to his already stained tunic.

'Now, let's see what's to be done,' the surgeon said heavily, pushing his bleary eyes close to the wound. He took a long probe from an inside pocket. McGaughey watched him, shocked, revolted. But there was nothing he could do.

11

Lieutenant Alabastor was still alive. He was on a mattress next to the door, so that the fresh night air might soon drive away the lingering ether fumes. Across from him were the two Indians, the older man sleeping silently, the younger, the man McGaughey thought might be his son, in a delirium, now the worse of the two.

Tired, depressed by what he had been forced to witness, McGaughey went and sat on the schoolhouse doorstep again. The square was filling. It was all being done silently, so as not to give warning to the sharp-eared Indians beyond the town. For the same reason, no unnecessary lights were being shown.

McGaughey saw the dim shapes of row after row of vehicles, and heard the tread of horses as they stood passively in the shafts. Everywhere men and women were scurrying, children cried, and there was the sound of adult weeping. There would be more, he thought, when relatives came to claim the seriously wounded. Many wouldn't be able to go, would have to be left behind to the mercies of the Indians.

He was trying to think about that, about a decision he must make, but all that ether had given him a headache.

'Comfortable, trooper?'

A thin-faced sergeant suddenly showed before him, the schoolhouse lamplight full on him. A bright-eyed, alert-looking man.

McGaughey looked up. His tone was cold when he replied. 'No thanks to you, Sergeant Gehler.'

Gehler. He did look different without that drooping eyelid. It made him look awake, more efficient.

Gehler's tone was hurt and he spread his hands in protest. 'How was I to know? You can't blame them Sioux on to me. An' this is a darned sight better than facing them Feds.'

McGaughey said, 'I'd take my chances down at Richmond right now.' His tone became vigorous. 'Talk about ungratefulness! And then telling Sara I'd sent for her. That's two you've got into this hole, darn you!'

But he was too tired to feel really angry. Back of his mind he was worrying about the wounded who would die if they were moved. Alabastor was one of them — he mightn't live till morning, anyway.

Gehler was grinning. 'That was real thoughtful of me, sending your gal to keep you company. Cost me five bucks.' His tone was injured.

The grin went from his face, remembering something. 'That's Sara Buie, ain't it?' McGaughey nodded. 'Funny thing, right after I'd got her out of camp there was a parade of all ranks on her behalf. Maybe it's something you ought to tell her.'

'Tell her what?'

'The Gin County marshal drove up

about the time you were leaving. A fellar named Henderson. He was making enquiries about a body that had been found drifting.'

McGaughey looked round into the night, but Sara wasn't there. 'Go on.'

'It was Frank Buie's body.'

'They're sure?'

'Henderson seemed sure enough to me.'

'All right, I'll tell her. She's been expecting bad news.'

The depression weighed even more heavily upon him. It wouldn't be easy, telling her. He thought, 'What do I do now?' He had his suspicions about Frank Buie's death. He felt he knew who was responsible.

'If I come out of Flagstaff alive I'll go and have a talk with Marshal Henderson,' he was thinking. Then he heard Sergeant Gehler speaking his name.

'Henderson had the hull darned regiment paraded so that he could talk to us.'

'About Frank Buie's death?'

'Not altogether. He did some talkin' about Frank's father, too. He got strung up by some lynchers.' McGaughey nodded. 'I don't see what he was gettin' at, but he wanted to know if any of our men had witnessed the lynchin'.'

McGaughey lost his tiredness, lost his depression then. Suddenly he was thinking, 'Tom Henderson's an intelligent man.' Tom Henderson wasn't the kind to waste his time.

'Did any man come forward?'

'Not a man. Couldn't have been any of our regiment.'

'No?' McGaughey was thinking back, remembering some things that had been said to him.

Gehler stirred like a man about to depart. He seemed tired.

'What's our chances on meeting a relief column?'

Gehler shrugged. 'I'd rather stay here. But it's Captain Hiss's idea to light out.'

McGaughey got stiffly to his feet. 'You don't like Hiss? What's burning into the man to make him always so darn mad?'

Gehler gently rubbed an eyelid that was probably tender. 'I don't know that I do dislike him.' His tone was slow. He was having to think this one out. 'I've known the Hiss family for a good many years now, and I reckon there's more to Berkeley Hiss than bad temper. He wasn't always like this — not as bad, anyway.'

McGaughey watched the sergeant narrowly. This didn't fit in with his opinion of the captain.

Gehler sighed and turned, and this time he was going. There was too much movement out there on the crowded square for an active man to stay apart.

'Yep, Berkeley Hiss has got a good side to his character. He's a man who knows a powerful lot about the word gratitude!'

McGaughey stared after Gehler as he went into the night. Then he shook his head. He didn't understand the man, not when he spoke about Berkeley Hiss.

But it was different, that matter of old man Buie, Sara's father. McGaughey stared at the crowding people in that square, dark and shadowy, and he thought, 'Sara will tell me if I'm right.'

Sara came up just at that moment when, for the first time, McGaughey was thinking, 'Maybe they came in with this company.' Three blue-chinned, hard-looking troopers. If so they might be in the darkness right now watching him. Then — Sara and Doctor Lockland were suddenly before him.

'We didn't get much sleep.' Old Lockland looked older than ever, more tired than before his brief rest. 'We were knocked up, told the town was being evacuated.' Lockland's voice was surprised, as if he couldn't understand the decision. But the military were in charge now, and Captain Hiss had made his decision.

McGaughey realised suddenly that most of the wounded who had been lying under the trees in the lamplit square had been moved already. But they weren't a problem; they would survive a wagon journey. It was these serious cases inside the schoolroom — over thirty of them. A few might be risked, but most would die if they were taken over rough trails in those springless vehicles.

A young civilian and a grey-haired woman who could have been his mother materialised out of the night. Doctor Lockland said, softly, 'This is the beginning. They've come to take Jack Klaus away and they'll kill him if he's moved.'

'And if he isn't moved?'

That set the pattern for their next half-hour. Relatives coming, being told they couldn't take their loved ones with them. Then the cries and tears, the pleas to be allowed to stay if their sons and husbands couldn't go from Flagstaff.

'You cannot help them by staying,' Doctor Lockland had to explain to them. He didn't need to add, 'It will be death — horrible death — for all white people found in Flagstaff when the Sioux come riding in, in the morning.'

There were meetings then, as the civilians tried to get the military to reverse their decision to evacuate the town. But many of the people were influenced by the cavalry commander's opinion and were for evacuation.

McGaughey could hear the arguments. 'We've got less than a thousand fighting men to guard the town and it's too big — too spread out. We were lucky yesterday, but the Injuns won't fight like that next sunrise. They want blood!'

'And there's seven or eight thousand of 'em now,' others added. Then a whisper pushed the figure up to nine thousand, and in a while everyone was believing in a force of more than ten thousand Sioux.

Even though it meant leaving a few badly injured, the decision to evacuate was adhered to. So it became a problem for McGaughey.

He and Doctor Lockland went round

examining the wounded, making decisions. Most of the patients were either sleeping or too far gone to understand what was happening, so making decisions wasn't hard.

They got away eleven who might reasonably expect to to survive the journey. When the two doctors came to the Indians McGaughey said with grim humour, 'The old one could stand the journey. Let's send him, shall we?' The younger Indian was raving, gripped in the fever of his infected wounds.

McGaughey looked at the hot, unnaturally bright eyes, saw the flush under the brown skin and thought, 'He'll be lucky if he lives.' Sara brought water, lifted the savage's head and got him to drink. But afterwards he went on raving.

After that there wasn't anything they could do. Alabastor was still unconscious, very white and bloodless. That crude surgery had shocked the patient, McGaughey knew, and he didn't give much for the lieutenant's chances of coming out of the ether.

All three went to the door. It was apparent that the move out had begun. Now there was a steady rumble of wheels, the quick grip of shod hooves as horses lurched into action. People were crying; overwrought parents were scolding frightened children. Wagon after wagon receded into the night towards the east road out. The square was becoming more open, less tenanted.

Lockland and Sara would be going in a covered wagon with some of the badly injured. Now they were lingering, reluctant to leave McGaughey, wanting to know what he would do.

'I'm a soldier.' They saw his tired grin. 'I wait until I get my orders. They won't be long in coming.'

He was thinking, but he wasn't going to let Sara know all his thoughts. As he walked with them towards the covered wagon he held her back for a moment.

'Just one thing you can tell me, Sara,' he murmured softly. 'Did Frank ever say how many soldiers he met running away from your blazing farm?'

If she said, 'Three,' that would clinch things in his mind. But she shook her head. She tried to remember, then said, 'No, I don't think he ever told me. Probably he was too frantic to notice.'

So he tried again. 'Did he say if they were infantry or cavalry?'

Again she began to shake her head, then she brightened. 'I remember now, he called them 'troopers'.'

'Cavalry.' Yet, though the county regiment was the only one stationed hereabouts, no man had stepped forward to say he had met Frank Buie that fateful afternoon. That was curious. Doubtless Tom Henderson was thinking so, too.

He brought his thoughts back to the present. The wagon on which Sara and Doctor Lockland were travelling was pulling into line. The horses reared, halted to let the last passengers get in with the wounded. Lockland was dragged over the tailboard.

McGaughey said, 'I'll lift you up,'

and swept the girl off her feet. She clung to him, startled because he had been sudden in his movements. He smiled down at her. There was little light here.

'I've earned this,' he said and kissed her and then set her over the tailboard. 'I'll see you when we stop,' he called, and he saw her vague form dissolve against the blackness of the interior of the wagon as the horses plunged away. She was looking back at him.

A trooper was awaiting him on his return to the schoolhouse. He was angry. 'Where in heck have you been? Captain Hiss says you've got to have the lootenant ready within five minutes. He's going to send a wagon to take him out.'

McGaughey told him, 'Alabastor won't see daylight if he's moved.' Not after that clumsy surgery.

The trooper was indifferent. 'I was told to give you a message. You've got it. I'm off.'

McGaughey went round his patients.

He was alone with them now. He adjusted bandages, noted pulse rates. Found a man had died suddenly. Then he came to Alabastor and saw the officer was conscious again. But he was in an agony of pain, McGaughey saw, wracked with it.

McGaughey stood by his side, looking down at the lieutenant.

'You're tough, lootenant. You came through better than I expected.'

For a second an answering smile touched those lips, then a spasm of pain contorted the face. But McGaughey thought, 'You're a fighting man, lootenant. Give you a chance and you will pull through.'

Only, taking him on a jolting wagon wouldn't give him a chance.

The young Indian was sitting up, his brown body, naked above the waist, glistening in the lamplight with sweat. McGaughey had to force him back on to his mattress. The man was rambling, raving, saying things in his tongue that McGaughey didn't understand.

He realised that something strong was attracting the younger man's attention and he turned to look. It was something to do with Alabastor, lying with his blue tunic spread as a blanket over him.

McGaughey rubbed down that hot, sweaty body with a damp cloth and it seemed to quieten the Indian who for a moment relaxed . . .

When McGaughey looked through the open doorway, on to that still-busy square, he knew he was being watched.

That came as a shock to him, because his thoughts had been on other problems and he wasn't thinking about danger to himself. He saw heavy cavalry boots motionless, facing him, at the extent of the spreading lamplight through the open doorway. The face and body were lost in the night's blackness.

But he knew who was the owner of those boots — what were their names? Binney, Collett and Feiner — one of them. For what other man would stand back and silently watch him so?

His fists bunched and he went quickly towards that door, fiercely angry. The feet turned and were lost in the shadows. When McGaughey got outside there was no one to see.

He walked back into the schoolroom, disturbed. His first thought was, 'I was a fool to go jumping outside. I might have stopped a bullet.' Then he dismissed the idea. No one of his enemies would openly shoot him — shoot him in a place which would leave no doubt that it was murder. That wasn't the danger.

The danger would come out on the trail, and it would not be for him but for Sara.

For *he* wasn't going with the townspeople.

12

He walked the length of the room, unseeing, for the first time not noticing the wounded. He felt impotent, helpless. Sara would be out in the darkness on that lonely trail. Amidst friends, and yet because she didn't know that enemies rode with her, she would be off her guard.

These men thought they had to kill her for their own safety. They would be able to do it easily in the night. Not with a betraying gun, either.

McGaughey felt jumpy. He went and stood in the doorway and peered into the square. Not many wagons remained at this end. He saw troopers walking through the darkness leading their mounts. These would be the rear-guard getting into position for the final ride out.

But he saw no signs of the three

hard-faced troopers who were so needlessly in fear. He began to walk to where a cluster of lamps showed where a control had been set up. A wagon plunged by, something was shouted by the teamster holding back on the long reins, and a man at a table made a note.

McGaughey stood and watched the check as wagons went through with little bodies of armed settlers marching guard behind them. Someone moved close up to him. He heard a voice, 'Gratefulness — gratitude. That surprised you, didn't it?'

It was Sergeant Gehler, thin of face, bright of eye, continuing as if time had not elapsed since talking about the Hiss brothers.

'It did. I've got no opinion of the captain, and just as little about that darned butcher of a brother.' McGaughey's voice was short. He was watching the officers. The self-important young lieutenants, for ever rushing into the night and barking a quick word of command. The N.C.Os, effacing themselves as they always did when it came to working before the captain's eye.

And the captain, staring like an angry-faced Napoleon to where the wagons were coming up. Finding fault, getting impatient. Getting things done, but doing it unpleasantly so that every man there worked with one eye on that red face.

And this was the man who held the virtue of gratefulness . . .

Gehler said, 'The butcher wasn't always like this, slow, old and dirty. I remember him when he was quite a fine, fit man. And not a bad man, either. You know what he did? He brought up Berkeley Hiss and the younger Hiss kids like he was their father, when their parents got drowned in a spring freshet that flooded a road one night. Yep, the butcher gave himself a hard life, taking on that family.'

'And Berkeley Hiss is grateful for it all?' McGaughey was contemptuous.

'Yep. Give that to Berkeley, he's done

everything in his power to repay that elder brother of his. Now old Ned's failing, Berkeley only works the harder to fix him in good positions. Like regimental surgeon — Berkeley fixed that for his brother.' Gehler sounded complacently pleased.

'He didn't get it for his surgical knowledge,' McGaughey said bluntly.

Gehler looked at him, his eye seeming very bright, the eye that had been hooded for so long. Softly he said, 'Ned Hiss didn't get a chance to go through medical school. He was too busy looking after an orphaned family. He learned his medicine the hard way, in his spare time when he was a man.'

'Well,' said McGaughey impatiently, 'it's not a good way. He didn't learn it good enough.' He thought of that unintentionally brutal surgery below the schoolhouse. 'You're being sentimental, Sergeant Gehler. Trying to make me feel pity for Ned Hiss and respect for brother Berkeley. But I don't. All I know right now is that a man might die very soon because of that family relationship.'

He went across to where Captain Hiss was standing. He had made up his mind now what to do. He had seen three familiar figures on the edge of the lamplight, watching him covertly from the ranks of other cavalrymen.

He sketched out a salute. 'No wagons come yet for Lootenant Alabastor — sir.'

Hiss began to shout angrily at a first sergeant. It became evident that that wagon had been overlooked. The sergeant went running round until he had found one.

McGaughey had got his story convincing, to himself, at any rate, by now. 'The lootenant's just out of ether. If he's moved right now for sure he'll vomit and that will start him bleeding again.' And that was true enough.

Berkeley Hiss was staring impatiently at him. 'Well, what of it?'

Gratitude. McGaughey was thinking

suddenly, 'Maybe if I played on that theme . . . '

'Lootenant Alabastor shouldn't be moved for another hour or so.'

'Impossible. We can't wait that long for him.' Berkeley Hiss was glaring at him.

'I'm not suggesting you should wait.' Hiss drew in his breath to explode. 'I'm willing to stay behind until he's fit to travel — sir.' He got it in quickly — 'He's a mighty fine officer, and I'll take quite a risk for him.'

The captain's anger subsided. McGaughey thought cynically that he seemed to have struck the right chord.

'Trooper, I'll leave that to you — and I'll remember your action.' Abrupt, unfriendly in tone, yet the nearest thing to being human except when his brother was concerned.

McGaughey stood there, feeling just a bit of a hypocrite, a humbug. Then he remembered the rest of his plan.

'I'll need help to carry him into the wagon. Some troopers, say. They could ride fast and catch up with the rear-guard once the lootenant was aboard — and I'd be up with the column within an hour, travelling alone.'

Captain Hiss turned to a first sergeant, who came to an agonised attention. 'Give him the men he requires.'

McGaughey began to turn. 'Three will be enough,' he was saying. He started to walk towards the cavalrymen, that sergeant by his side. 'I know the men I want.'

'Get 'em, then,' a relieved sergeant said, glad to have an excuse to get away from the captain.

McGaughey walked among the silent, waiting troopers. 'You, you and you for stretcher detail,' he ordered, and Troopers Binney, Collett and Feiner went rigid with shock at being singled out.

McGaughey began to walk away. 'Send 'em up with the wagon,' he called over his shoulder to the sergeant. He had detailed them. He knew they would have to come. This was one way of making sure that no harm came to Sara in the night.

He had to work quickly now. He ran across a square that was littered with belongings jettisoned at the last minute from overloaded wagons. When he leapt up the schoolhouse steps he saw that the young, delirious Indian had crawled from his mattress and was trying to get round his father towards Alabastor, on the opposite side of the doorway. The older Indian was painfully trying to stretch down to restrain his son.

McGaughey took the young warrior under the armpits and gently dragged him back to his mattress. 'You quit galloping around,' he reproved. 'You'll do yourself harm.' He couldn't understand what was attracting the Indian so powerfully, and he hadn't time to find out.

The older Indian had stretched himself and was watching him through partly closed eyes. McGaughey winked at him then went down below.

Swiftly he attended to wounds that needed fresh bandages, gave drinks where required and left water to hand, though most of his patients weren't able to help themselves. But it might be hours before he could get down to them again.

One more settler had passed out, and another — quite a boy, with stomach wounds — wouldn't last much longer. But the dead had to remain for the moment with the near dead.

He went back upstairs. Halting, he heard the rumble of wagon wheels approaching, the clip-clop of shod horses heading this way. He went round the schoolroom fast, this time leaving water to hand only. Then he got his rifle out of a cupboard, went to an empty mattress behind the young Indian, lay down and pulled a blanket over him right up to his eyes. The rifle felt cold against his bare arm, lying there.

Eyes almost closed, McGaughey watched that doorway. About him men stirred and groaned. Below came a sudden harsh sound — it would be the end of that boy, he thought. Then the Indian began to sit up in bed again.

'Blast him,' thought McGaughey. He didn't want the wounded Indian to get up to any tricks now . . .

Someone was outside the doorway. McGaughey could imagine a man standing out there, listening, looking in, hand gripping a gun, suspicious.

Then all at once three men were standing just inside the room, rifles held ready, watching all ways at once. Troopers Binney, Collett and Feiner, of course.

They looked quickly round the schoolroom, saw wounded men on mattresses and at once turned their attention towards the lighted stairway that led below. There was no other door leading out from the schoolroom.

McGaughey saw the Indian fall back, as if exhausted. The movement brought eyes round at once. He was glad he hadn't begun to crawl out of his blanket, and he cursed the Indian again.

The three troopers were moving towards the stairhead. They went two or three paces on tiptoe, then stood in attitudes of listening. At length they were at the top of the stairs. A whisper and all began to descend.

Then McGaughey came sliding out of his blanket and caught them while they were strung out down the stairs. There wasn't much room there for men to swing round with their rifles, and because he could look down upon them they couldn't screen each other's movements. He had them completely at his mercy.

His voice cracked the silence over that lamplit cellar. 'You — get those hands above your heads! Guns and all!'

There was a cry from one of the men, the cry that tells of nerves stretched to breaking point. A snarl from another. Three faces leapt round to look up at him. Scrub-faced for lack of a shave. Eyes widened, sharp, bright and fearful. Mouths working, saying inarticulate things.

A moment while they looked quickly round, looked at each other. Hoping for a way of escape, hoping that a companion would make a break for it and draw fire.

Then three rifles were raised above three bleached blue cavalry caps. Three men stood crouching on the steps, waiting for the worst to happen.

McGaughey snapped, 'One of you kicked me, remember? All of you pitched into me with your fists. Remember that, too? Now, you murdering, lynching lice, crawl up these stairs and see what's coming to you!'

Again they looked at each other. Again they waited for a companion to leap into action. The moment passed. Binney — or was it Collett or Feiner? McGaughey thought — began to ascend those worn stairs.

When his hand came level with him, McGaughey snatched the rifle out of it and tossed it on to a mattress. When the next man rose level, he was disarmed similarly. Then the third.

McGaughey said, 'You'll be safer on your backsides. Sit against that back wall, sit a couple of yards apart. Then keep on sitting.'

Without turning his eyes from the trio, McGaughey pulled a hard-backed chair against a wall. He sat on it, tilting so that he was leaning against the wall on two legs. It was comfortable. His rifle rested easily on his lap. He could shoot the first man who moved. They would get him before he had time to reload his single-shot Martin, he knew, but he also knew that neither Binney, Collett nor Feiner would move. All the same he wished he had a repeater such as the Sioux were reported to be using.

The Sioux. The older warrior, only a few yards away, was watching with expressionless eyes. Behind, the younger warrior in his delirium was pulling at the bandage around his thigh. 'He won't live long if that comes off,' McGaughey found himself thinking. He wouldn't be able to do anything about it; he couldn't take his eyes away from that trio.

Time passed. After a while there was no sound from outside save for the restless cavalry mounts and the horses in that wagon. After the steady bustle of the past hour the silence was chilling, repellent, disturbing.

McGaughey saw the sweat on the faces of those three men, sitting straight-legged against the back wall. The lamplight fell from above them, making shadows where their eyes should be and on the lower part of their faces. But he knew they hadn't looked away from him for a second since he had shouted down those stairs at them. They would be away from that wall in a flash if he relaxed his vigilance.

After a very long time, with only that silence now where three thousand people had so recently been, a harsh voice struggled from the throat of one of the men. The man on the right, the man who had led the way down those stairs. Perhaps the boldest of the trio, the leader.

'What about the lootenant? We was told to fix him on a wagon.'

McGaughey shrugged. 'I've changed my mind. The lootenant will die if he's moved. So he won't be moved.'

'You won't be needing us?' It was a weak attempt at bluff.

McGaughey said, 'I won't be needing stretcher bearers.'

'Then we can go?' The men were straining to watch McGaughey's face.

'Sure you can go.'

McGaughey lifted the gun slightly, so that the barrel covered the spokesman. He made no attempt to rise. McGaughey saw him lick his lips.

'You can't keep us here.' The voice was harsher, more strained than ever. 'The darned Sioux will be in the town soon . . . '

'The darned Sioux will find us here,' McGaughey said gently.

That moved them. In spite of the rifle it brought them rearing up against the wall, all talking, shouting at once.

'We're not stopping for any scalping. You're crazy to think of staying!' It was the man on the left, the man at the rear of the column that had descended those steps; the man who had cried out in fear, whose nerves were worse than his companions'. His face was twitching; he was panting. Only then did McGaughey realise how much of an ordeal life had been for these men in recent days. But this was no time for pity.

'Shut up, you carrion,' he ordered, his rifle jumping viciously. 'These men are sick and want rest.'

They slumped back — it was comical to see how quickly they got down on to their seats against that wall again. He saw the gleam of their eyes as they stared at that mencing rifle barrel, could feel the swift intake and then the holding of breath as it pointed at each in turn.

But they continued to talk. Was he mad? Did he want to lose his life? What had he got agen them?

The rifle jumped again. There was a hint of latent savagery in that swift movement, and it wasn't lost on them. They stopped talking. McGaughey said, gently, 'That's better. I don't want noise. And I'll do the talking.'

But for the moment he was content to sit on that tilted chair and stare across the lamplit room at them and listen for night sounds outside. He was tired, wanting to sleep, not wanting to talk, not wanting to exert himself in any way.

But he couldn't sleep, didn't dare. And there were things he wanted to know, to be sure about before turning these men over to their death.

He sighed, drew a deep breath, and then said, 'Tom Henderson came to Gin Barracks a few days back.'

The three sat in silence, only their eyes glistening in the shadows of their brows revealing a new tenseness. Looking at them he thought, 'Why did I think they were all alike?'

They had seemed indistinguishable

as personalities until now — blue-chinned and hard-faced was how he had always remembered them. But looking at them now he saw differences — this one on the right was thinner-faced, probably blue-eyed. The middle one had a softness to his chin that rounded it under its stubble, he had thick, fleshy lips that were never closed — a mouth breather. And the man on the left — the dangerous one because he was bolder, the apparent leader — had a broad face, shiny across the cheekbones; he had eyes that seemed recessed in the bony structure of his skull. And he had a mouth that snapped close into a straight hard line after he spoke.

McGaughey said, 'When Henderson asked for some men to come out — men who had seen a lynching some weeks before — why didn't you own up?'

That man on the right spoke. His voice was toneless. 'Because we never saw no lynching, that's why.'

McGaughey didn't mind. There was plenty of night before them, many hours before the Sioux came creeping into this deserted town.

Patiently he said, 'No, you never saw men lynching old Buie . . . you lynched him yourself.' That man on the right, thin-faced, nervous, cried out a denial, began to say things, perhaps too much. The middle man snarled through thick lips and quietened him.

'Yes, you went to that lonely farm.' They'd have been watching it for days, maybe, once they'd got their crude plot in their minds. When they saw that the girl was away and the boy helping a sick neighbour, they had gone swiftly in. 'It was planned, cold-blooded murder. You went straight in, got old Buie and hanged him.'

They weren't talking now, were just staring at him. Crude, callous brutes who would take a life so that whisky could flow down their throats.

The older Indian was watching impassively, not understanding a word that was spoken. Then McGaughey realised that a patient, a man with an amputated hand, was awake, that his eyes were upon him and without the brightness of fever. Here was a witness — if he lived to tell the tale. McGaughey shrugged. He wasn't bothered about witnesses, only with knowing the truth.

'Now, why should you want to hang a hard-working family man?'

That man on the left spoke, the man with the lights glistening on the high-drawn skin across those high cheekbones. His words were cunning. 'Buie was a darned Reb. Rebs deserve what they get. Not that we did anythin' agen the old fellar.'

'Why burn his house, though?' McGaughey spoke as if sure these men had committed that crime. 'Buie was a thrifty man and there are no banks hereabouts. His savings would be hidden in his home. You had found his hiding place — did you torture him to get the secret from him?' he asked quickly, suddenly. It would be like these men.

That Indian was trying to sit up again. With these three snakes to watch, he didn't want any distractions caused by a feverish patient.

'You got his money.' That was why Sara and her brother had been living in a primitive river cottage — because there'd been no money left to them. 'Then you fired his house so as to hide the real cause of that lynching — robbery. You left that poor old man dangling for his son to find and ran away.' Hot anger stirred at the thought. It had been horribly callous, indecently brutal. And all to get a man's few dollars.

'You'd planned to say there were lynchers at work if you ran into anyone. Well, you did — you bumped into Buie's son. He, poor lad, believed your story, so that afterwards everyone went looking for lynchers who didn't exist.'

He let a few more seconds go by. There was no hurry. His tired brain was going slowly into the sorting of this problem, yet he felt he was dealing with it efficiently. Gently, watching them all the time, he asked, 'What did it feel like, afterwards? When the days went by and you read in the papers that Marshal Henderson was trying to find some mythical lynching party?'

They would have been jubilant, gleeful. Getting drunk on the stolen money in celebration of a successful coup. That was how they would react — there would be no remorse, no stirrings of conscience. Only fear for their own safety affected men like these.

But then had come something to shock them out of their complacency; all in one moment their safety had been rudely disturbed, shattered.

Frank Buie had recognised them.

'One day you were in town on duty — it was when the draft selectors came in. You had money in your pockets; you went off to spend it, to get liquor inside you.

'That was the biggest mistake you

made. You were quite a bit drunk when Frank Buie suddenly stood before you. If you'd been sober you might have bluffed things out, but you weren't. So you made a mistake. You struck him down — as if that would rid him as a threat to you!'

He could imagine the three, arrogant because they had got away with a crime that had filled their pockets. Fuddled with alcohol. And seeing Frank Buie before them, asking questions. Panic. Swift fear vomiting into action. And that action — to strike out at the face that seemed a threat to them.

Only, it had been needless, unnecessary. Probably Frank didn't suspect them; for if he had he would certainly have said so to his sister. No, there must have been some reason other than accusation, suspicion, that had brought young Frank away from his sister's side.

Tom Henderson, of course. McGaughey snapped his fingers. He was tired or he would have thought of it before. Very tired. Lie down, you goldarned Indian!

Why don't you rest, sleep; I would in your place.

'What did Frank Buie say to you, there on Main Street?' The trio sat in silence, not replying. 'Probably you don't remember. But something to do with Tom Henderson, I'll bet.'

Henderson had been out to the riverside cottage many times, Sara had said.

He jerked his head erect. He'd almost been dozing, he realised — and those three killers had realised it, too. They were waiting for him to sleep, to leap forward and grab his rifle. Then they would kill him because he knew too much, and afterwards Sara would be the next target for these frightened men.

'Thought I was sleeping, eh?' he jeered, and they seemed to sink back, baffled. Tom Henderson? Oh, yes. Tom was clever. Tom hadn't been satisfied about that lynching. Tom would naturally say to young Buie, 'Those soldiers. Could you recognise them again? If you see them, get them to come to me. I'd like to talk with them.'

'Frank Buie said, 'Tom Henderson, the marshal, wants to have a word with you.' ' McGaughey looked at the man in fear on the right and knew his guess was good. That must have been an awful moment for the men, to hear Tom Henderson's name on Frank Buie's lips, to hear him saying, 'Henderson wants you.' No wonder they had panicked, lost their heads — betrayed themselves irrevocably.

Frank had been struck down. Perhaps his head had hit the stone roadway, adding to the injury. At any rate, Frank had been bemused, dazed, concussed, hours later.

'You'd had too much to drink. You couldn't think clearly. All you knew in your panic was that Frank Buie had recognised you, that he was the sole witness who could connect you with that crime at the farmhouse. All you could think was that Frank Buie had to be got out of the way.'

And yet he was sure they could have bluffed the boy in some way; it had all been so unnecessary.

'When you got Buie outside the Enrolment Office, what did you do? Crack him on the head and then drop him into the river?' That sluggish river which hadn't carried the body clean out of the county but had left it bobbing about in the vicinity of Gin Point. Maybe it had been stuck for days under the wharves, he thought . . .

His head jerked erect again. Wakefulness returned fully, suddenly. That man on the right, the thin-faced man, the man who looked gaunt in that lamplight with the black stubble sooting his face. He was talking, words were falling from his twitching lips. He'd been in hell since Frank Buie had shown up that sunny morning on Main Street.

'We didn't kill him. You're wrong. He just died out there.' The other two were reaching across to grab his shirt, to shut him up. They were swearing, their raging anger directed against this weak comrade of theirs.

'He just died, I tell you. We didn't kill him. When we put our hands on him he just dropped and we saw he had died all of a sudden!'

And that was the truth of it, McGaughey knew. Knew it because the man was in too great a terror to lie, knew it was the truth because otherwise those other blackguards wouldn't be trying to shut him up . . .

Frank Buie had been dying all the time he had been sitting in the sunshine outside the Enrolment Office. Head injuries were curious. A man looked to be all right, looked to be getting better, one minute; the next there was blood in his brain and he was out of this world.

Poor Frank. Dying and no one knew it. Dying even while his sister wiped the blood from his lips before going on her business in the town — and then meeting him, McGaughey. She'd spoken her mind to him, filled with indignation because of the way her brother had been treated . . .

McGaughey said, 'All right, you didn't kill Frank Buie then, outside the Enrolment Office. But you'd struck the death blow an hour or so before. You killed him there on Main Street. Who struck the first blow?'

His eyes were on the man on the left, the leader. But the others didn't speak.

McGaughey sighed again. Still hours to dawn — and the Sioux. But he knew what he was going to do when they came.

'You realise that in admitting as much as you have, you've admitted to everything else I've said,' McGaughey said gently. He looked at that patient across the room. The man was still listening, was understanding. The Indian was crawling again, moaning, moving his head almost like a dog questing for a scent. He was down by his father's feet and trying to come round.

The spokesman of the trio said harshly, 'We never admitted to nothin'. When Buie fell ill in front of our officer we took him outside to get better. That's all we know about him. We'd never seen him before, whatever you think. He just died on our hands.'

'Then why come back and say he had run away?' The man shifted uncomfortably. 'Why drop him into the river?'

None of the trio spoke. Their wits weren't quick enough to save them. They weren't intelligent, thought McGaughey; and then he wondered if he was, for sitting there under those circumstances.

'You beat me up.' His tired brain groped with the problem. Then he saw why it was, how it had happened. They'd been watching, had seen Sara Buie leave her brother and go straight across to McGaughey. To the trio it must have seemed as if she was speaking about the incident, about the assault by the three troopers.

They'd come across to him, had smashed into him with feet and fists. It was the only thing they could think of, their brains befuddled by drink and panic. They had thought to intimidate him, to keep him from interfering by thrashing him. It was crude, brutal, ineffective psychology, the reaction of animal brains to a situation delicate and demanding a finesse beyond them.

But he could understand them, sitting there now in that yellow lamplight. That first reaction to blinding panic had created a chain of events binding them to the hideous past. With every blow struck afterwards they had brought fresh disaster upon themselves.

'It wasn't smart, any of it. Not smart at all to kill old Buie as you did. For you're going to die for it.'

The weaker one of the trio seemed to whimper and his hands moved ineffectually. McGaughey was thinking. 'The Sioux camp will be waking now.' On the war trail they'd be preparing for the fight an hour or two before dawn. But there'd be no fight when they rode in; only McGaughey and a lot of wounded would be there to receive them. These three killers wouldn't be there . . .

Was there anything else? Yes, that night when the floating body had been reported. One of them had overheard the report; all three, perhaps, had gone quickly down before an ambulance could be prepared and had shoved that body out into the current.

Then, because the fear of death was upon them, they had gone right away to find Sara and quieten her — Sara who had been seen up at the barracks only that same day, frightening them. But he, McGaughey, had ridden up before they could could get into the cottage.

McGaughey said, 'When Henderson showed up at the barracks I'll bet you sweated pints!' He liked to see their fear; they should suffer before they died because they were evil and had brought only suffering to others in their lifetime.

13

The leader of the trio reared to his feet suddenly. His mouth was so tightly indrawn that it must have been painful. He had lost his temper, lost some of his fear in consequence.

'You keep on talkin'. But what good does it do? If it's all true what you say, how's that goin' to help you? You don't want to die when them Sioux come, do you?'

'I don't want to die. Maybe I won't die.' He'd like to live because he'd told Sara he would be seeing her again, and he wanted to see Sara once more. She would make a good doctor's wife when this war was over, he thought . . .

'Then let's get away — all of us. Our hosses are outside.' The tone was eager; the sweat was on that face again. Those other two were rising, crouching and watching him.

'And the wounded.'

The leader shrugged. 'What can we do for them if we stay? Just a few more people will die.'

McGaughey smiled. 'I stayed to look after the wounded.' That patient seemed to have gone to sleep now. McGaughey could speak out. 'They've got no chance if they're moved, but there's hope for some of them if they can rest here and get treatment.'

'The Sioux — '

'There's still hope, a chance. You never know, even with savages.'

'And you'll risk your life for such a slim chance?' The man's tone was rough, incredulous. He refused to believe it, because it wasn't a thing he could see himself doing.

McGaughey shrugged tiredly. 'I'm still going to try my hunch.'

'Well, I'm not.' The man was going to try a bluff. He was desperate. He took a pace forward. 'I'm gettin' out of here before them varmints come.'

McGaughey sighted down the barrel

of his rifle. 'It's on your stomach. I can't miss at this range, brother. And dying with a bullet through your guts is the most painful way of going out.'

The man — Collett, Feiner, Binney, whatever he was named — came on. His foot lifted to take another stride. His companions were easing up from the wall. There was a tight grin on that stubble-face.

'It's got but one bullet, that Martin. You fire it an' my pards'll tear the life out of you!'

McGaughey's trigger finger took first pressure. 'That's true. But the second your foot touches ground you'll have lead in your guts. Go on, brother, see if I'm bluffing!'

The foot descended. Then it halted, hovering. The grin went off that face. There was weakness suddenly, the weakness of a man not sure — a man suddenly appalled at his nearness to death.

Then that foot went back to its companion.

McGaughey ordered, 'Sit down, all of you. You're not going yet. I'll tell you when it's time to move.'

He didn't speak in the next two hours, but his rifle never wavered from those fearful men.

Dawn was a long time coming, and then all at once it was with them. Haggard men looked at each other in a brightening light that made the oil lamps worse than useless. Outside birds flew with quick fluttering wings and called to each other, marvelling at the deserted town, then complaining because there wasn't the usual food about.

McGaughey saw the grey light through a window over the heads of those three killers take on a yellow glow. Then it was all gold and hot sunlight streamed on to his face. He had to shift his position so that he could watch those men without having the light in his eyes.

The room warmed immediately. It wakened the wounded. There was stirring, groans and quick cries as pain stabbed anew at them. Men tried to lift, tried to look round and understand. Some saw him and called to him, but he shook his head. They would have to wait. But not long now. Downstairs a man was shouting. He would have to wait, too.

Those killers were desperate-eyed now, even that bolder, more spunky leader. They were fidgeting, growling to each other, their growls coming sharper, taking on a higher note.

The Sioux must be watching the town now; must be closing in on it, puzzled by its silence. McGaughey thought, 'They'll have warriors all round the town again.'

Now these killers could go. He didn't want them around any more, wanted them to be away before the Sioux came riding in. Sara was safe from them now, safe forever more. Justice would be done.

The killers would never escape with their lives.

McGaughey let the chair crash on all four legs. There were pins and needles in his limbs, but he forced them into action. He stood across the mattress on which were their three rifles; his own pointed unwaveringly at the trio, startled into silence, into rigid inaction at his movement.

'Your hosses are outside,' he told them. 'I don't want you any more. Go — if you want.'

'The Sioux.' That leader, mouth like a rat trap, but eyes panicky. 'Give us our rifles.'

'Don't be a fool. Would I live if I let you have them? Get out!'

His own gun swung. That nervous man broke into a stumbling run towards the door. Then the other two followed. McGaughey came to the doorway and looked after them. They were flogging their horses like crazy men as they went across the littered square towards the east road out.

The east road. He shrugged. Sharp-eyed Sioux would be on that road, reading the signs of departing white folk. The trio would run into them. The thought made him satisfied. It seemed to him that all this was right and as it should be. The world was better without men like Binney, Collett and Feiner. He wished now he had asked who was who, but it was too late. Too late and unimportant.

His tiredness was still upon him after his sleepless night, yet it seemed supportable now that day had arrived.

He pumped water out in front and came in with filled buckets. He took off his shirt and thoroughly washed his head and body. It felt good, afterwards, with his hair slicked coldly close against his scalp. The tiredness went; his brain felt alert. That was how it must be; he would need to be vigilant in the next hours. All these lives depended on him.

Then, very quickly, he went round to his patients. He rebandaged where stiff black blood made old bandages useless. He held up men and gave them water. A few wanted food and he gave them fruit and some bread he found in a woman's basket. They wouldn't harm for want of food or drink for a while longer.

Some were conscious, asking questions. He didn't withhold the truth. 'You're all in a bad way. I couldn't risk moving you. You've got a chance while you lie here and rest. So . . . here you are. The others went out in the night.'

'But them Injuns?' a haggard, almost bloodless man asked, his eyes staring.

'They'll come.' McGaughey shrugged. They were probably inside the town already. 'I'm just hoping they won't kill you.'

Someone very weak from wounds began to weep, to upbraid his people for leaving him. But most took the situation philosophically. It had happened time after time in the history of the West. The weak had to be left so that others might survive.

McGaughey went to the doorway again. He had given the same attention to the Indians as to the other men. The older Indian seemed much recovered; his brown eyes looked calm and level, his forehead was cool. But he could barely move because of the raw wound in his throat that had nearly run the life out of him, and he was still weak from loss of blood.

The other Indian was worse. McGaughey had an idea now the man might die. His wound on his thigh was messy, running with pus. His face and body were hot to the touch, and he was never still. He was quiet for long periods and then he would begin raving. Then he usually started to try to move round the foot of his father's mattress.

Alabastor was either asleep or unconscious. He looked very white and ill. He might die, but he was strong and could make it yet, McGaughey thought. No one could tell.

Now he put those three rifles against a chair facing the doorway between Alabastor and the older Indian. He brought up another chair beside it and sat down. Then he waited.

The wounded, those who were conscious and with the strength to be curious, watched every move. Then someone called, 'Why are you stayin'?'

McGaughey thought there was a movement down an alley opposite. He dragged his eyes away reluctantly, tried to think of his answer. Found truth on his lips.

'I couldn't leave you. Not after cutting you up and doctoring you and fighting to save your lives. No. I found I couldn't go with the others.' His eyes were back across the square. There *was* movement. 'So I thought I'd stay — '

'An' die with us?' A hoarse, incredulous whisper.

'I thought maybe none of us would need to die. I've been trying to balance in my mind, to see if there's a chance of life for us. I still think there is. At any rate, I'm willing to take a risk on it.'

There was a long silence, the silence of exhaustion. Every man who could was thinking, thinking of the next hour or so. After a time someone in a corner called out weakly, 'This pain I'm in, it don't matter if the Sioux do come. I can't suffer more.'

After that no one spoke until the Sioux came.

McGaughey knew they were in the town; probably scouts reconnoitring to make sure there wasn't a trap laid by the cunning white man. He had hardly seen a movement, yet he could feel a stirring all about him.

Finally, there was a sound outside, a sound no greater than the velvety rustle of bats' wings, and a Sioux stood before him in the doorway.

A big warrior, like most of the Sioux. Naked save for a breech clout. Body painted in red, white and black. Circles. Triangles overlapping. Wavy lines. And crude. Frightening at first, but almost instantly looking childish.

The face was the same. Lines of paint sweeping across from the nose, red on a background of white. Black to prolong the mouth and make big the eyes.

He stood there, crouching, a new rifle gripped in sinewy brown hands. It was pointing at McGaughey instantly.

But McGaughey, sitting there, was resting the muzzle of his Martin against the bare ribs of the older Indian.

The wounded inside that schoolroom looked at the Sioux, bulking there in the sunlight of the doorway. The wounded Indian looked beyond the bandages round his throat to that gun in his ribs, then quickly looked at the standing Sioux.

McGaughey sat almost negligently, one leg cocked on top of the other, watching the war-painted brave.

The warrior's quick eyes darted round the room, saw the wounded whites and Indians. He seemed about to step forward. McGaughey shoved the rifle barrel and made the wounded Indian gasp. That stopped the Sioux.

He understood. He made no effort to come forward now but after a few seconds vanished as soundlessly as he had come. Then McGaughey relaxed.

He withdrew that rifle and said to the older Indian, 'Sorry, pard. Didn't like to make you jump like that, but I had to stop that Injun.'

That Indian. He would be one of the scouting party. When time passed McGaughey guessed they had gone back to their people to report the town deserted. Soon they would be flooding into the place, looting and destroying. That was all right so long as they didn't get up to tricks with his schoolhouse, he thought.

He shifted on that hard chair. There were barrels across the square. He was uneasy about them. They seemed to have been set outside a shop deliberately.

Sometimes white men did that when retreating from a settlement — left broached casks of whisky to tempt the raiding Indians. Only, strychnine and arsenic had usually been added by bitter, vengeful whites. If that were so; if Indians died horribly after drinking poison, nothing would hold them back from the schoolhouse, not even the life of their fellow.

So McGaughey sat and watched those barrels in the sunshine and hoped they were nails and not liquor.

With an abruptness that made him think he had come out of a dream, that square suddenly filled with crazy, careering, jubilant Sioux. He saw them swing down from their ponies, saw them break their way into stores and houses. Loot! That would keep them occupied for some time. He was only uneasy about those barrels, wished he could see what was happening over across the sunlit square, but now there were too many ponies in the way . . .

A party of Sioux chiefs came riding slowly in front of the schoolhouse. They swung down from their saddles deliberately, without any hurry. Then they came walking towards the doorway.

McGaughey put the gun back into the Indian's ribs again. This time the warrior didn't flinch at the touch of cold metal, merely looked at the trooper with inscrutable eyes.

McGaughey leaned back in his chair and without any flicker of expression on his face watched the Indian chiefs come to a halt a yard beyond the doorway. He looked from one painted face to another. Now, though, he never saw the paint. War paint startled you at first, but right afterwards it was as though you didn't see it; you looked for the man behind and focused upon him.

That was the way it was when a man had a scar on his face or a big nose. At first you could only look at it. Then you never saw the disfigurement . . .

A chief spoke suddenly, his voice harsh after the long silence of that room. The younger Indian seemed to recognise that voice for all his delirium and he came rearing into a sitting position on his mattress with a suddenness that startled everyone. McGaughey saw those hot, feverish eyes in that fever-flushed face; saw blood seeping from the bandage around the Indian's thigh and knew the artery was bleeding unchecked again. But his glance was distracted only momentarily. Then his eyes came back to those chiefs in the doorway.

Chiefs were dangerous men. They took risks to distinguish themselves. He didn't want to present his scalp, and all these wounded's, to some quick-footed, honour-seeking chieftain.

The older Indian replied. McGaughey didn't understand it, but it seemed very casual. A grunt. A few words. The faintest shrug of those bare, brown, finely-muscled shoulders.

The chiefs conferred among themselves. All the time one or the other watched McGaughey, almost lounging on that hard, wooden seat. They wouldn't go away. They wanted to kill these white men, yet they couldn't do it because of that gun that would first destroy their own comrade.

That, McGaughey knew, was what was holding them back. Not any sense of gratitude for having treated their wounded comrades with as much care and attention as if they hadn't been enemies. A few, he thought, might have felt generous, but always in a body of men were some mean enough to do anything, any time, under any circumstances.

It made him think of Collett, Binney and Feiner. They would be dead by now. He knew it, it was how he intended it. Unarmed, they could never have broken through that encircling ring of Sioux. He felt no regrets.

Then he thought, 'When will some Sioux come riding in to say the white men are escaping into the hills?'

Revenge was a stronger motive than loot. When they knew how and where the white men had gone, every Sioux who thought himself a warrior would be out of that town and on the war trail within minutes. It would divert attention from the schoolhouse, though it turned the danger into the fleeing column.

Still, he thought, looking at the angle of those shadows, the settlers were getting a better start than they had imagined. For certain they would be fifteen miles away by now, off the plain and climbing into the hills. If only they could keep ahead of the Sioux until they ran into the relieving force . . .

The Indian chiefs were baffled. They were angry. McGaughey didn't like to see them angry, for men in temper behave unpredictably . . .

That danged Indian was crawling across the foot of his father's mattress again, he realised with shock. That Indian talk in the doorway seemed to have roused him, to have given him strength. He was running blood on the floor as he moved.

And then McGaughey realised two things. The young Indian wasn't heading for the doorway — he was crawling now towards the unconscious Alabastor.

And the Indian was armed.

14

There was a knife in the young warrior's hand. It was tiny, so small it could have been hidden in his breech clout all the time. With the cunning of a sick man he had kept it to himself until now. Now he intended to use it.

The chiefs were crouching there, watching — hopeful that something would happen now which would permit them to come running into the schoolhouse and kill the white men.

The young Indian was behind McGaughey's chair. He couldn't see him. And yet he knew he was safe, knew it was Alabastor who was to be the Indian's victim.

McGaughey eased upright on his chair. He knew he couldn't sit there and see his lieutenant stabbed to death under those circumstances. But it seemed he could only stop this crawling

Indian with the madness in his brain by killing him.

And if he killed him, he knew nothing would stop that avenging rush of those red men outside. Nothing.

There was no sound now in that schoolroom. Some of the wounded must have understood the extent of the drama and were watching, hanging on to their breath . . . wondering how McGaughey was going to handle the situation.

He was sweating. Trying to watch everyone at once.

Then he got up, his gun still pointing at that Indian with the throat wound. He backed to Alabastor's bed; took the blue officer's tunic with the silver 'C' for cavalry buttons on it and hurled the garment at the feet of the Indian chiefs.

The young Indian was on his feet. In him would be a strength astonishing for a dying man, McGaughey knew. He wouldn't have been disarmed easily.

But now there was no need to disarm him. He staggered past McGaughey's chair. He was moaning, but now his face was draining white. It was that hated officer's tunic that had been attracting his feverish attention. His eyes were still on it, unheeding the helpless lieutenant. He took two strides and then fell on his face. Blood began to collect under him.

'He'll die if he isn't attended to right away,' McGaughey said to that older Indian, but he didn't get off his chair.

The older Indian lost some of his calm. He said something to the chiefs, quickly, urgently. Indicated his son, now still and quiet.

But the chiefs didn't move. Those brown appealing eyes came round to McGaughey. He shrugged helplessly. His gun never moved. The Indian father began to crawl off his mattress. McGaughey could kill him; he wasn't going to see his warrior son die before his eyes.

McGaughey knew the thoughts in that Indian's mind, knew and respected them. But again he was losing control over the situation and those Indian chiefs knew it. If the older Indian warrior was prepared to invite death, some chief among them might take advantage of it . . .

There was a scream somewhere across the square. McGaughey's instant horrified thought was, 'They've strychnined a barrel of whiskey!' Then he realised it was a rallying cry from some great chief.

Instantly those chiefs by the doorway wheeled and leapt on to their ponies. From every alley braves came running in toward the square. There was noise, shouting, the shrill whinny of rearing, bucking ponies, movement. And the movement was towards the east road out.

Word had at last come back to the main body of Sioux. The fleeing settlers' trail had been found. Now every Indian wanted blood, not loot. Now they were storming out of the town with everything forgotten but the enemy out on that open trail before them.

There was a stillness over a square more littered than ever. The birds came back and made their song. The sun blazed yellowly down upon a town twice deserted in a matter of hours.

McGaughey got up. He went outside and looked around. When he was sure no enemy remained, he set down his rifle, took hold of the young warrior and turned him over. Deftly he rebandaged him, then dragged him back to his mattress.

'Hell, you nearly gummed up everything,' he panted, but he looked after the man as well as he could for all that.

Then he helped the older Indian on to his mattress. 'You weren't much better, either,' he grinned. There was no change of expression on the Indian's face, no gratitude. McGaughey thought, 'If he felt it would help him, he'd slit my throat in no time.' He had no illusions about warriors taught from birth to believe that an enemy should be killed, and to be unscrupulous was to be a warrior among warriors.

He brought water for the Indian and then went his rounds of the other patients with his rifle slung on his back. But the Sioux didn't return. The fight was now miles away from Flagstaff.

* * *

It was two days before the cavalry rode back to Flagstaff. Two days of pursuit of an enemy routed by the unexpected intervention of two regiments of infantry.

Captain Hiss turned that red face of his towards the distant rooftops and wondered at them. The Sioux must have ridden out in a mighty big hurry not to have set fire to the town first, he thought.

Back on the trail they had found three mutilated, scalped troopers. Feiner, Collett and Binney. He remembered them as HQ staff. Bad soldiers, not even clean. But he didn't like the way they had gone out.

It made him think of Lieutenant Alabastor and the Harvard-educated Trooper McGaughey. McGaughey who had killed a woman, according to his brother.

That was why McGaughey wasn't in Erlington County and wasn't practising as a doctor any more. The fellow had had to get out with his life.

He shifted in his saddle. Patients did die under a doctor's knife. Too many died; too little was known about surgery. And people always swore the surgeon was a butcher and a murderer under those conditions.

What was it Ned had said? Poor old Ned, failing fast, worrying the life out of him by this physical and mental degeneration. Ned who had been a father to the family all those years.

'He shouldn't have operated. It was risky. He should have let the woman die.'

A woman with powerful friends and

relatives, with a a husband who could use the law, such as it was, against the young doctor.

'If McGaughey lived I'd never have mentioned it to him,' Captain Berkely Hiss thought. 'I might even have recommended him for a commission. Men like that are needed.'

Men who stayed behind to give an officer a chance to live. Only, poor Alabastor and that McGaughey fellow must have died with the three troopers even though their bodies hadn't been found . . .

When the cavalry trotted into that littered square they saw a pipe-smoking man sitting on a hard chair by the schoolhouse door. Their astonishment was beyond expression. Then they saw a man waving from a mattress just within the school-house, a man with an officer's tunic on his blanket: it was Lieutenant Alabastor.

Officers and men fell out of their saddles to get across to the tall trooper.

They were shouting, asking questions that couldn't be answered by any one man in a matter of minutes.

McGaughey slowly rose from the chair. He knocked out his pipe. For two days he had been a bored man, wanting time to pass until this minute. And now it didn't seem important because the cavalry had been first to return and not the settlers.

For Sara might have returned with the settlers. His heart leapt to think of it. Sara would return to look for him, he knew. She needed him now because she was alone and lonely. And in these past two days he had decided that he needed her, too.

Captain Hiss was looking down at him from his saddle. McGaughey remembered to salute. Then he realised that a report was expected from him. He collected his wits.

'Four men dead in your absence, sir. One an Indian. The rest coming on fine.' Especially the lieutenant. He rubbed a weary limb, and then distinctly they heard him complain.

'Sir, it's cruelty to make children sit their days on chairs as hard as this. No wonder kids hate school!'

Other titles in the
Linford Western Library:

SPARROW'S GUN

Abe Dancer

Before setting off in pursuit of his father's murderers, Will Sparrow must learn how to handle a gun . . . Miles away from home, he plans his reprisal while working as a stable-boy. But then Laurel Wale happens along, and Will discovers his intentions aren't quite as clear-cut as he thought . . . Meanwhile, his mother has settled down nearby with one of the territory's most important citizens. She wants nothing more than peace — but nothing is going to deter Will from his fateful objective.

BLACKJACKS OF NEVADA

Ethan Flagg

Five years in prison have given Cheyenne Brady plenty of time to dwell on revenge after being left for dead during a hold-up by the Nevada Blackjacks. Upon his release Brady joins up with an old prospector, Sourdough Lamar; together they head for Winnemucca and the prospect of honest work. But when Brady's old gang, led by Big-Nose Rafe Culpepper, plans to rob the town's bank, Cheyenne is accused of masterminding the hold-up. Can he extricate himself from once again sinking into a life of crime?